INTO THE MYST

JORDAN CHIPPER

CONTENTS

1

PROLOGUE

Eliza Rose was thinking a dark and perilous notion as she stood in front of her home. She said beneath her breath, her voice coloured with a mixture of fury and despair, "I'm going to kill my mother today."

She was often irritated by the circular glasses her mother had purchased for her. Eliza already dealt with a lot of abuse and mocking at school, and the spectacles only made things worse.

With each passing school day, the pain from the frames pressing into the bridge of her nose grew worse. She knew she would strain her eyes trying to see through the lenses, and she knew she would have a headache.

Her shoulders were burned by the leather rucksack straps as the hot sun beat down on her. It was a hot day that signalled the beginning of summer vacation. Her thick hair was blown across her face by a strong wind gust, impairing her vision.

A fellow student abruptly sped past her and shoved her roughly. When he turned around, he was giggling hysterically with his companions and pointing at her face.

They all joined in, making fun of her glasses while pointing. Eliza lowered her eyes, returning their attention with a scowl that was filled with rage. Her mother's passing was on her mind at that precise moment.

Eliza inhaled deeply and bit her lip to try to force a smile that she hoped would be genuine. Her focus changed when she saw Miss Canary, her next-door neighbour, fiddling with her plants. Eliza's mother had been chatting to her a lot more recently.

Eliza was momentarily diverted from her melancholy thoughts as Miss Canary gave her a friendly wave as she looked up from her musings. Eliza occasionally found peace in the forest and field that were located behind Miss Canary's house.

Eliza brushed off her experience with her classmates and turned her attention to the roadway in their neighbourhood that was dotted with homes. She calmly waited for the crossing guard to stop the flow of traffic so she could cross without risk while tucking her hands into her pockets.

She paused at the bottom of the stairs as she got to the front of her house and sighed with exhaustion. However, the door squeaked open as she went for the handle.

She took Eliza's rucksack and whispered, "There you are," with relief in her voice. "I was going to meet you on the street right then. You don't want to spend the entire day outside in the heat, I'm sure. Step inside. Her mother's grin was warm and welcoming.

Eliza's mother cast a quick glance in that direction, her smile giving way to worry. Her worried expression was seen in the tightening of her lips and narrowing of her eyes. Eliza wondered why Miss Canary was watching them, so she turned around to see her. The neighbour gave a quiet nod before stooping to tend to her garden.

Eliza's head was filled with contradictory feelings as she could tell her mother was uncomfortable. She went inside the house with her mother, who escorted her into the living room. Eliza waited impatiently for her mother to respond, desperate for some sign of acknowledgement or connection.

What has been going on lately? Eliza at last spoke up, unable to keep her curiosity in check. Her attention shifted to the subtle tattoos on her mother's arms. And why do you persist in attempting to hide your tattoos? I'm 14 years old. My generation, I believe, is aware of them.

Eliza's mother appeared to ignore Eliza's remarks as she moved over to the couch. She started out by saying, "There are a few things I need to tell you," with a mixture of reluctance and resolve in her voice. And now seems to be the ideal time to do it.

Are you going to die? Mother of Eliza shook her head, her eyes filled with unspoken sentiments. The question "Do you have cancer?" She denied it once more while making sluggish, tiny movements. "Okay, well. I don't need to be here with you, down here. Eliza moved away, her strides dragging with annoyance. "I need to start my summer homework."

Her mother spoke first, a hint of fear in her voice, "Bad people are always around us.

Eliza gave a weary nod as she turned around. Mom, I'm aware. She went to the kitchen in the hopes that a food would provide comfort.

"Eliza, be quiet and pay attention to me. This is significant.

Her mother pursued her quickly, grabbing hold of her shoulders, and turning to face her directly. Her mother's eagerness cut through her diversion, and the enticement of the fridge started to lose its appeal. She took something that resembled a sharp knife with a delicate silver handle out of her purse. I'm holding a dagger. To be safe, I want you to carry it with you at all times.

Eliza scowled, her dissatisfaction clear. "Why can't I just have pepper spray or something normal?"

"Because doing this will benefit you more. Eliza, you're not a typical adolescent. You are extraordinary, able to do things that most people can only dream about.

Eliza asked, her face wrinkled with confusion, "What do you mean?"

Her mother glanced up at the ceiling for a split second before returning to her daughter. Your being a witch.

A glint of happiness appeared in her eyes as her smile grew wider. Eliza, though, was unable to smile of her own. Who aspires to become a witch? Not her, for sure.

Eliza's heart skipped a beat as she came to terms with the realisation. Except for the constant ticking of the wall clock, everything appeared to stop around her, enclosing her in a crushing quiet. Her disbelief became stronger with each tick-tock, grating on her nerves.

You can't possibly be serious.

"It's up to you whether you believe me or not."

It would just serve as yet more justification for people tormenting her if word got out that her mother thought Eliza, Eliza Rose, was a witch. There were whispers of uncertainty that her mother was going insane. She was not going to believe any of it.

Witches weren't real; they were merely made-up people from stories or animated films, the products of people's imagination. While it's true that her mother used to read her night stories, she is now fourteen and disparaging her intelligence won't assist her mother's cause.

You're claiming that I have supernatural abilities, then? Do you honestly believe I'm so easily duped? With her lips pursed into a tight line, Eliza responded.

"I don't, no. The optimum time to reveal a witch's child's actual nature, though, is when they are in their teenage years. Her mother's voice shook, her eyes darting to the door behind Eliza as terror overcame the momentary joy she had earlier shown. Prior to it being too late.

before it was already too late? It appeared as though her mother was reluctant to discuss what was to come. She shouldn't have bothered her with this information if it was obviously sinister.

Eliza was sorry her mother had admitted to being a witch. She thought back to all the times she had overheard her babbling about mystics and broomsticks downstairs. She had snuck out of her room to listen in but every time she had heard her mother chatting to herself.

Particularly, one recollection stuck out clearly.

Eliza overheard her mother tell her imaginary friend standing in front of the bookcase, "They're in the crowd with humans," from the top of the staircase. How else am I meant to safeguard the defenceless? Her mother had fallen to the ground abruptly, and the air was thick with the pungent smell of burning.

Eliza's mood had deteriorated. Her mother looked up, astonished to see her still awake, as she hurried down the stairs to check on her. Her mother's odd countenance from that evening resembled the one she has now.

Introspectively tracing the floor, her mother's gaze. She turned back to the bookcase next to them, the same one with which she had previously conversed. Eliza couldn't get rid of the feeling that her mother had a mental condition of some kind.

"What makes a witch... a witch if I don't have any special abilities and can't cast spells? You got me these spectacles so I wouldn't be teased at school, and now you're accusing me of being a group of spooky witches? Eliza's voice sounded both frustrated and unsure.

While clutching the blade firmly in her hand, Mom's lips pursed and her brows wrinkled. She rummaged through her purse with a playful grin on her face. After a brief pause, she produced a thin, brown object with the same silver lines as were on the knife. On its surface, a tiny red button was glowing. Eliza raised her eyes, her expression marked with perplexity.

She exclaimed, "Mom, what the hell is that?"

When she looked up, her mother's eyelashes fluttered. This is your broomstick, my dear.

Eliza staggered backward and hit the wall behind her as a result of being caught off guard. Her vision was hazy as a result of her spectacles falling to the ground. She was overcome with panic as she hurriedly searched for her glasses.

She reapplied the accustomed cold frames to her face as she struggled to restore her calm. She took her mother's rucksack and sprinted passed her. Her respiration accelerated despite her mother's efforts to calm her down. From the perplexing form in front of her, she moved back.

Her mother said, "You must be home by eight now, and it is very necessary to keep your broomstick with you wherever you go.

Eliza disregarded her mother's advice and ran for the front door as she yelled, "Eliza, kindly return. Although there is a lot to process, everything is for your own benefit.

She grunted loudly while covering her ears, slammed the front door behind her, and dashed outdoors. As Miss Canary, their next-door neighbour, watched Eliza storm out of her home, she stopped what she was doing and her face showed confusion.

Asking, "What are you looking at?" Eliza snapped, trying to gather her thoughts as the day turned into night. She then sprinted along the pavement. The neighborhood's old playground was located at the end of their street and was mainly deserted because of tales of nighttime monster sightings in the nearby woods.

Eliza, though, was unconcerned about the woodland. Maybe she was different after all.

Rusted chains squeaked above her as she sat down on a swing. She didn't swing hard, but the noise irritated her ears anyway. She put her hands over them and got off the swing. Her fingers were snaked by the wind as it whistled and tickled the tip of her nose.

Her backpack fell to the ground, revealing the broomstick and dagger within. Eliza shook her head and spoke a foul phrase.

Before I went, Mom must have slipped them both into the bag.

She picked up the items out of curiosity and studied the broomstick's design. Her finger accidentally depressed the red button, lengthening and adding a little weight to the broomstick.

Eliza's mouth dropped open as she pondered what was taking place in front of her as the silver lines carved on its surface started to shine. Eliza instinctively tucked the broomstick back into her backpack after a streetlight that was close to the playground broke into pieces.

She was intrigued and turned to the disturbance, drawn to the sound of breaking branches and rustling leaves coming from the woods nearby.

Could this be the terrifying creature everyone has been speculating about?

After turning, she focused on a pair of piercing yellow eyes. She rubbed her face and blinked many times, half expecting the eyes to disappear when she opened them again. Instead, a mesmerising variety of blue and green replaced the yellow orbs. They emerged from the shadows, accompanied by a plethora of colourful flecks.

The ethereal sparks gently swirled through her surrounds, beckoning Eliza to follow them. She stepped carefully, worried that anyone seeing her near the shattered streetlight could think she was to blame. She pushed aside the glass pieces and discovered no signs of purposeful harm.

A tall, curiously dressed man dragging a woman into a dark alley next to the road suddenly caught her attention. The man appeared to be in some degree of disarray—his torn shirt and pants—and he was determined to lead the woman deeper into the shadows.

The trail of vibrant dust he left in his wake served as a signpost as he quickly glanced behind him for any pursuers. Eliza stayed out of his sight, invisible to him.

The man grasped the woman's exquisite frame with loving hands, causing her to smile and chuckle. He then shifted his attention back to the alley. Eliza stooped and tucked her black boots into which the dagger was hidden.

Her muscles woke up from a surge of energy, and she felt tingles from her head to her toes. Her arms and legs began to get goosebumps, and she shuddered. She blinked many times, trying to make sense of her disorientation.

Even though she couldn't remember moving a single step forward, she couldn't help but feel drawn to the alley's entrance. The park became a blurry background when she turned around.

She pursed her lips in an effort to gather her thoughts, but she soon realised that she was no longer in control of her thoughts. She was drawn towards the dark lane by curiosity.

The couple's apparent joy and pleasure filled her with a deep desire to feel the same. Anything that may momentarily take her mind off the chaos in her life seemed worthwhile.

She wondered if it would be harmful to indulge her curiosity when her life already felt like a train wreck. Why not try to escape the thoughts of her trying times at school? Why not temporarily ignore her father's absence? She was intrigued by the man's intriguing allure as well as the alley's dark, spooky atmosphere.

Her lips parted in reaction to the enticing aroma filling the small area in front of her. She struggled to release a stray middle finger that had become stuck as she carelessly swept her fingers through her thick auburn curls. Because of the stress of her worrying biting, her lower lip trembled.

Above, the gloomy clouds began to change into terrifying forms. She moved further down the alley, her urge to find the couple growing as she thought about various things.

The girl's voice echoed, "Stop, you're so silly," and her contagious giggles drew Eliza in even more.

A blast of wind caressed her cheeks with a chill as it scratched against the dim path's walls. Her nostrils were overwhelmed with the intense aroma of newly cut wood and lilies, which made her nose twitch.

With each step she walked, the glistening guide that had initially lead her to the alley began to disappear as she turned around. Her ears were brushed by whispers from the jungle, but nothing appeared.

As she made her way farther into the alley, she could hear the sounds of two people sharing a passionate kiss as the gravel crunched beneath her boots. She became persuaded that she was getting closer to where the pair was. She carefully adjusted her small glasses in an effort to keep them from falling off her nose.

As she moved forward through the cramped area, she noticed a dim light. The girl's skin was covered in colourful glitter that fell gently upon her like dog drool. As he kissed the girl again, his lips dipped down towards her collarbone.

His back was covered with bright, pointed wings that fluttered excitedly. He hung slightly above his unaware target, increasing his hold on her waist as he reached inside her blouse.

The girl's body's veins started to shape themselves as she pressed her hands up against the wall. The creature's greedy stare shifted to the girl's neck, his next intended victim.

His wings' hues glistened and blended in the shadows, reflecting unsettlingly on his flawless skin. His body was covered with intricate, curling tattoos, each with a distinct vibrant colour. They lit up and moved down his bulky neck. His desire to taste the girl's skin was apparent as his piercing icy black eyes focused onto her. She had an unperturbed face of confusion that appeared drugged.

A colourful cloud of dust engulfed them both as his wings landed and glided neatly through the restricted area.

Eliza lowered herself to the ground and carefully and precisely pulled a silver knife from her black boots. She tenderly held it between her thumb and index finger as she thought of a strategy to save the girl.

"Mystics, disguised among the people," her mother muttered, echoing in her head. Her focus sharpened and fixed on the creature in front of her.

She forced herself to get up and run to the girl's aid. But her heart fell into her breast, her throat became dry, and her hands curled into shaking fists.

She was frozen with anxiety, unable to leap forward. Her eyes raced from left to right in search of a solution as anxiety etched her face.

Her attention was drawn downward by a sound, and as she looked down, she noticed that weeds were growing up her legs from the ground. She felt a shudder run through her as the wet mud rubbed against her flesh, giving her calves an excruciating sting.

Her senses were dulled when a soft breeze from the creature's wings caressed her face and carried an alluring aroma.

She felt drowsy, which clouded her eyesight and made her lose motivation to help the girl. She discovered herself frozen in a bizarre tranquilly. Her thoughts were occupied by the scent of fresh roses, which directed her behaviour.

She tried to wake herself up by blinking, but when her eyelids grew heavy, she gave in to the tranquilly and stopped trying to fight it.

It felt wonderful.

Eliza's movement was restricted as the weeds wrapped around her legs and proceeded to climb. She shook her head, trying to get her bearings again. Her lips were pursed shut as she concentrated on carefully cutting the plant strands.

Her motions and reflexes slowed down with each slice. It appeared that the aroma had caused her nervous system to react in an odd way.

She covered her nose and silently toiled away at the weeds with determination. But the growth beneath her grew stronger with each cut. She was further fixed in place when the gravel turned into a thick muck.

Eliza's heart raced and her lips dried out in the midst of the girl's deafening groans and the approaching weeds. The creature's strong hold on the girl allowed it to caress her battered body while leaving glowing imprints on her flesh.

The creature gave her another colourful hickey as the sinewy weeds slithered around her neck and colourful drool dripped from its razor-like fangs. Eliza was tempted by the sensation of its tongue lazily gliding across her neck. She discovered that she was as frantically longing for the creature's touch as its defenceless prey.

Consider it, Eliza. Maintain your attention.

She shivered as the chilly wind played with the little hairs on her skin. The beast stopped and turned to look at the girl as the groans subsided. It kept looking at where Eliza was hidden. She accelerated her cutting in an effort to quickly liberate herself. Its grin grew, exposing sparkling crimson lips that had been hidden by shadows.

The beast floated slowly in the direction of Eliza, allowing the weeds to completely engulf the girl and preserve her as a future feast. It held out its palm and weed and root tendrils sprung up from the ground and twisted around Eliza's ankles and neck. Then, after slapping across her mouth, they snaked up her thighs, muzzling her shouts.

Eliza raised her dagger and attempted to cut the weed covering her mouth while leaning against the wall, much like the girl before her. However, her grip slipped, and the dagger fell to the ground.

She struggled desperately to breathe out of panic, but the alluring smell kept filling her nostrils and overwhelming her senses.

Her heart rate dropped sharply as she kept staring at the floating, grin-sporting monster. Her emotions simmered, and calmness crept over her with the touch of its gentle palm against her flesh.

Her turn had finally come, as her heartbeat skipped.

CHAPTER ONE

Eliza struggled for breath, coughed, and desperately searched her face for indications of her death with her hands. She searched for a solid ground underneath her, tightening her fingers on the dewy grass.

Her throat was dry and itching, and she had a pounding headache. Her heart was thumping in her chest. Since her father abandoned her and her mother, she had been haunted by these terrifying dreams.

Eliza eventually gave into sleep's embrace as her eyelids started to get heavier.

The fine grass blades in the swaying field swirled and whispered in time with the light air. As the morning progressed, the calming sound of rustling leaves caressed her ears and serenaded her.

In this field, Eliza frequently went in search of comfort, lying down and letting the soil hug her. She watched the sky as it changed from the dark blue of night to a brilliant blend of orange and crimson from this vantage point.

Massive clouds invited her to observe their majestic passage as they slowly crawled across the heavens. She stretched her index finger into the sky, playingfully slicing through the unseen air, her nails digging into the damp, soft dirt. She adjusted her spectacles and then focused on the woodland in front of her.

The inviting branches appeared to be whispering a request.

Eliza's eyes would close whenever she was tired or deeply thought about something, and the same constant nightmare would take over. A beast carried the woman along the foreboding alley in this terrifying vision, filling her senses with a gruesome spectacle.

She was able to see, touch, hear, and smell every terrifying aspect in the nightmare because it was so vivid that it felt like the present. Her mind was plagued by the unfinished puzzle and the piece that was missing.

Being a witch included nightmares as a burning side dish and a constant sensation of déjà vu. Eliza stood up and took one more look at the ominous woodland. She then started down the road that went back to her house. The field served as her haven, where she could tackle the troublesome ideas that had troubled her as a young adult.

She instantly realised that this was her first day of college classes. She took out running down the dirt path, passing Miss Canary's house in a blur. She crossed the street quickly, oblivious to any notions of traffic safety, narrowly escaping a passing car. Adrenaline was pumping through her veins as she sprang forward and landed in front of her house.

She quietly opened the door and shuffled upstairs to gather herself before addressing the outside world. A startling loud cry broke the air as I climbed into the bed in her chamber.

Her cat, Jared, emerged from the tangled covers and leaped onto the ledge with ease. He focused on Eliza while methodically grooming his nails. He then cast a quick peek at the alarm clock, which was still beeping hysterically.

That was pretty rude, he said after a dramatic pause. His ear twitched in annoyance. "Eliza, I demand a sincere apology."

Eliza rolled her eyes and rushed to her drawer after adjusting her untidy hair. Her room was transformed into a disorganised sea of bras and shirts as clothing flew randomly in all directions. Socks fell on Jared's shaggy head with every ferocious rummage.

The alarm clock briefly stopped its clamour, only to pick up again a short while later. That clock had a clear malfunction, and it was bound to stop beeping shortly.

Jared fell from the shelf after hitting his head against the windowpane while being totally hidden by a pile of socks.

Oh, the stench! He cried, "You killed me. Do you ever organise your wardrobe, lady? He continued, sniffling, "It's positively revolting." He jerked his head to the side, knocking a sock off, then crashed into the bed while muttering obscenities.

Eliza was too busy looking for something decent to wear to pay much attention to Jared's misery. The nightmare she had in the field had left her with a throbbing headache, the feeling of prickling weeds on her skin and a racing heart. However, after the nightmare was over, she remained emotionally numb and cut off from her surroundings.

Eliza realised she couldn't save the girl, and she had to concede that her hopes were in vain. She was rendered helpless to save anyone as the monster's scent overpowered her. Despite her best efforts, the scent of new wood and grass took control of her mind, making her feel helpless and frail. The creature's obscenely dark eyes stuck in her head like an unbreakable melody.

She began to worry that she was becoming insane.

She initially considered telling her mother about her worries and getting assistance from a mental hospital. She might be brought back to her senses with a dose of reality, along with a speech about appropriate witch etiquette, broomsticks, and her untidy hair. Eliza understood, however, that she would never actually carry out such a plot.

She glanced at her phone to check the time and saw she was already running behind schedule for her first day of college. She didn't frequently arrive late, though occasionally she might. She was irritated when the alarm clock, as is its nature, started beeping again.

She complained, looking for anything appropriate to wear, "Where is it?"

"For the love of God, Liza, turn off that miserable clock of yours."

She murmured under her breath, "Shut up, Jared."

With a trace of mischief in his voice, he joked, "Not even a 'Jared, you're so wonderful?'"

She gave him a sour glare as her eyes started to close. Hissing in response, he made it apparent that he was angry.

Jared, her feline companion, was a familiar—a being that support-ed witches in their magical work. Unfortunately, her familiar was more likely to be lazy than to be helpful. He complained, whined, and dozed off all day.

With her thoughts elsewhere, she staggered into the loo and promptly forgot to fetch her chosen outfit. She quickly decided on a flowy yellow cardigan, a simple brown cami, and a pair of white shorts. She sighed deeply and quickly gathered the clothing before returning to the restroom. She hastily dressed, but a loud crash resounded from within before she could open the door.

She hissed, "Jared," with tight teeth.

She swung the door wide with a quick motion while keeping her gaze fixated on him. He gracefully jumped back onto the windowsill after kicking the ticking clock to the ground. Her snobby cat started to rub his plush white back against the window.

"What? He honestly protested, blinking, "I did nothing wrong.

She snatched her handbag and asked, "Really?" with her anger clearly audible in her voice.

He remarked, lazily grooming himself and flicking his thin tail over the edge, "I mean, I did instruct you to turn it off.

Jare, that's the third clock you've managed to ruin, she yelled, turning to walk out of her bedroom.

You constantly say that, but you didn't witness me shatter it. He yawned, "Where's the evidence, hmm? Will you deliver me to an animal shelter?

She glanced at the shattered clock and muttered, "That wouldn't be such a bad idea," before crossing her arms over her chest.

He looked down at her bare feet, "It's okay, blame the cat," he said.

She became aware that she had neglected to put her shoes on. Why was she so forgetful? She went looking for a pair of shoes after tripping over a sea of bras while trying to get to the closet. She hastily slipped on a pair of adorable white flats that she had never worn.

"Those are purrfect, and your cardigan goes well with your light green eyes," he said.

She mumbled, "Thanks," as she observed her image in the large mirror leaning against the wall. Even though she didn't think anyone would ever notice, she changed her clothes and pulled up her nonexistent cleavage.

Hey, at least she was trying, right?

A crooked grin appeared on her face as she blinked at her mirror. She attempted to grin while exhaling while rubbing the area of her nose where her spectacles frequently caused skin irritation.

The college she intended to attend, which was not far from Centreville, Virginia, where she now lived, was the same one where her mother received her degree.

She was aware that she might miss her first class if she didn't leave right away. However, college was probably less rigid than high school. Finally, she would be leaving the nest on this chilly day. She was filled with excitement, yet she also had resistance.

Although she had to go for school, she wasn't really eager to. She would rather spend the rest of her life on the couch, binge-watching Netflix until she was eighty years old. Jared jumped into her bed with style. She started to leave her room but ran into the door.

Glasses," he mockingly said. "Do I have to protect you at all costs?"

She whirled back to face him and pursed her lips. She then moved her glasses to the shelf on which they were always stored. As she carefully put glasses on, she felt the familiar comfort and her vision immediately became clearer. Jared jumped to the foot of her bed, and she could now plainly see the letter 'J' dangling from his collar.

She said, "You're a lifesaver," and threw her purse over her shoulder.

Yeah, you don't know, he said in a condescending manner.

She smiled at him as she ran down the stairs after leaving her room. She almost fell. In the kitchen, she discovered a letter on the table in the middle that read:

arrived at work early. A bagel is on the table. If it's missing, Jared probably ate it.

PS: Recall your broomstick.

Be careful.

-Your wonderful mother

The arrow on the note naturally pointed in the wrong direction.

She yelled, "Jared!"

His voice rang out from her room, "You weren't going to eat it anyway. He obviously knew about the missing bagel. He infuriated her, and she shook her head.

The purpose of the broomstick as a weapon was previously known to Eliza. It was the exact weapon she had seen at the age of fourteen, intended to destroy the enigmatic monster. She was disappointed to find that the broomstick would not work for her, giving out merely a soft glow and a warm sensation when touched. Eliza was concentrating on education even though she knew she would ultimately learn how to harness its power.

Eliza methodically looked through the kitchen in her desperate hunt for her broomstick, her eyes darting all over the space before she moved on to examine the rest of the home. Her sense of urgency grew as a result of its obvious absence.

The broomstick had a distinctive look, like a spinning baton with a button in the middle and silver lines encircling its cylindrical form. Eliza could change its size by pressing the red button, which was occasionally accompanied by a mysterious radiance. Surprisingly, the broomstick's slender and compact construction allowed it to slip without difficulty within her pocket.

Eliza was unsure about the broomstick's exact use despite its link with witches. It was very different from the idea of a flying broom seen in fairy tales.

Eliza was unable to confirm or dispute Jared's assertion that witches were not at all like the characters in popular culture.

Although she thought witches were incapable of casting charms, Eliza's mother insisted that she was a witch. In her quest for self-knowledge, Eliza had discovered fascinating information about what it meant to be a witch. For example, she now knew that Jared was her familiar and that she and her mother both had broomsticks.

Despite Eliza's developing suspicion that the broomstick had no practical use and that her mother could be losing her sense of reality, her mother had insisted on the necessity of always having the broomstick close.

Her mother had said, "It's a weapon," but Eliza had trouble understanding how it worked and could see no usefulness in it. Jared had added, "It will reveal its power when the time is right," but a long time had passed with no sign of the broomstick becoming a terrible, imposing weapon like a chainsaw-gun or a deadly slasher.

Eliza's doubts about their assertions grew over time.

Eliza was moving across the living room when she came across the bookcase and experienced an unexpected occurrence—a warm breeze touching the tip of her nose.

She looked about curiously, locating the source of the air behind the massive bookcase. Eliza peered closely at the building because she had a creepy feeling that something supernatural was going on there.

When she was there, the books on the shelf frequently displayed odd behaviour. Eliza saw that they were moving and making noises, but everytime she tried to grab them, they avoided her, giving her the impression that the bookshelf was really haunted. It was covered with a thin layer of dust and gave off the impression of having been neglected; it was obvious that her mother needed to spend some time organising the books.

Eliza delicately ran her fingers over the book bindings while blowing on the wooden surface to try to remove any dust. A sudden loud thud reverberated throughout the space.

Eliza's broomstick was lying on the ground beneath her feet, much to her surprise. Her eyes automatically turned to the bookshelves where she noticed fleeting silver swirls emanating from one of the covers.

A green book and a purple book that intermittently captivated her peripheral eye with their illusive light were left behind when the colours quickly faded due to her fast blinking. But no matter how hard she tried to look at them, they always stayed steadfastly commonplace.

She took her broomstick out of the ground and held it in her hand. Eliza's finger lingered over the button tucked in the centre as she looked down at the well-known item and said softly, "I'm sorry, broomstick." The broomstick's silver lines lit up as she pressed it, and there was a tiny scraping sound as it shrank to fit neatly inside her pocket.

Jared shouted from upstairs, "I accept your apologies! Eliza, it means so much...seriously.

Saying "Shut up, Jared."

He retorted, racing downstairs and stopping at the doorway, waiting for her. "Your apology is so sincere, and I really do appreciate it!"

Eliza stroked her auburn strands with her fingers and stormed out the door, rolling her eyes at Jared's criticism. She left their dwelling with her broomstick safely tucked away in her pocket and turned to the street sign. They were located close to a busy road, which was flanked on the other side by a series of brick townhouses.

Eliza and her best friend Dawn had decided to move in together because they both found the campus dorms to be unsuitable for their purposes. For the time being, renting a condo looked like the best option. Later that day, her mother had proposed possibly paying a visit to her new home.

Her mother had recently been preoccupied with a challenging endeavour and was living a very chaotic existence. As a result, Eliza had decided against making her responsible for going with her to school. With the help of the crucial GPS navigation, which had never let her down before, she felt confident in her ability to find her way to VCU.

Eliza also wanted to avoid herself the emotional outbursts of her mother. Such situations could be frustrating because her mother's emotions were frequently irrational.

She was aware that her departure represented a crucial turning point for her mother, who struggled with the knowledge that her little witch was growing up and leaving the carefully crafted cocoon of safety. Eliza raised her head, let out a loud breath, and looked towards the entrance.

Miss Canary, a strange individual whose quirks paralleled those of the haunted bookshelf, lived across the street. Even though Eliza had little interaction with her, she was nonetheless remembered for the early childhood meeting.

"Eliza! Dear, come meet Miss Canary," her mother had urged.

Eliza burned her fingers on one of the books while playing with the ones on the shelf. Her mother quickly grabbed her up and brought her to the front door as tears started to build up in her eyes. A woman was standing outside on the porch, clutching a flower that still had its painful thorns. She didn't appear to be bothered by their existence.

Her mother reprimanded her, "What have I told you about touching those books, honey?"

As her mother carefully laid Eliza down on the ground, the scent of freshly cut grass and fallen petals filled Eliza's senses. Leaning forward to introduce herself, the pale woman stood.

She said, "Hi there. My name is Terese," opening her silky pink lips to expose a row of pearly white teeth. What is your name, too?

Eliza, who was clutching to her mother's leg, gave her a dubious look. Be courteous, honey, her mother stroked her on the head and urged.

She mumbled, "Eliza," as she came into Terese's direct line of sight.

Terese asked, "And your last name?" Eliza furrowed her brow in response. Looking behind Terese, she saw a young child with his bright green eyes fixed on her, looking out from behind the half open door. Eliza redirected her gaze to Terese and said, "Rose."

The woman appeared to have been expecting Eliza and smiled warmly at her when she saw her. She said, "Ah, I thought so," with her eyes sparkling. She handed Eliza a rose in a gentle manner, her smile widening, "This is why I brought this just for you." It's a unique rose since the thorns won't prick you.

Eliza gave the rose a puzzled glance. She questioned, "But... thorns always hurt,"

Eliza spotted a young child playing nearby, holding a stem of a flower. Undeterred, the lady continued, "This is a rare flower from the forest behind my house." One red petal abruptly broke off and floated elegantly to the ground. The boy grinned mischievously at Eliza as he quickly tucked the flower behind his back. The woman's eyes had a knowing look as she transferred her attention between the two.

Eliza finally managed to say, "Thank you," a mixture of appreciation and perplexity in her voice.

Her mother greeted Miss Canary and then closed the door as Eliza ran back into the home while holding the rose in her hand. Murmuring sounds outside became more furious and louder. Then, Eliza's heart began to pound in her chest as a loud crash against the door resonated throughout the home.

She carefully placed the rose on the bookshelf only to watch as it suddenly caught fire and turned into a pile of red ashes. She became overcome with rage and grief, slumped to the ground, covered her face in tears, and cried.

The family cat, Jared, caught wind of her grief and sprang up onto her lap. Eliza, who had never owned a cat before, found refuge in Jared's steely blue eyes and soothing purrs, which helped to progressively lessen her suffering.

Eliza's feelings gradually waned in intensity, and she started to lose track of the rose and the commotion outside.

Even though time had gone, Eliza's recollection of Miss Canary's gift remained. She couldn't help but see Miss Canary every time she went outdoors, her familiar form seemingly unaffected by time. Her poise was enhanced by the blonde hairdo on top of her head, and she always waved politely while looking at Eliza.

But what really captured Eliza's attention was the woodland beyond Miss Canary's home. This particular woodland, in contrast to
others in the region, radiated a calming atmosphere, with leaves
that revealed secrets and a setting that delighted her senses. Eliza
frequently daydreamed about giving in to the forest's seduction and
finding another elusive and exceptional rose.

The breeze played with Miss Canary's black sundress, which was
embellished with yellow canary blossoms, on a nice day. Her delicate skin was bathed in sunlight, which highlighted the little freckles
that danced across her arms. Her delicate motions reflected the
elegance of her dress, and her pointy ears provided a subtle hint
of otherworldliness.

In an effort to find her car keys, Eliza combed through her purse.
When she found them, she pointed them in the direction of her car
and pressed the button until the recognisable beep indicated that
the car was opened.

Her mother gave her this car for her sixteenth birthday, and it
represented memories and the passing of time. She sighed as she
realised she had grown from a teen to a young adult. Jared was
tucked away in the backseat among the mess, soundly sleeping as
shown by his regular breathing.

Eliza started the vehicle after slipping into the driver's seat and
turning the keys. Eliza's hand appeared through the sunroof, imi-
tating guitar chords while Taylor Swift's well-known voice filled the
air, singing "I Knew You Were Trouble." She enthusiastically sung
along, relishing the occasion as if she had written the song herself.
Her voice soars.

While stuck in traffic, Eliza carelessly twirled the ends of her
hair, letting the breeze play with her hair because the window was

open. Her automobile turned into a private performance venue as the music blared. Her attention was drawn when a black sports motorcycle came up next to her.

She resumed her wild dance routine, waving everywhere, oblivious to the motorcyclist's interested glances. She accidentally pointed her finger in the direction of the rider.

Eliza was startled to learn that the stranger had seen her embarrassing act, and her cheeks began to flush red. She looked at him with a mixture of shyness and self-consciousness. She was temporarily out of breath as he winked, revved his motor, and expertly steered through the gridlocked traffic.

When a car horn behind her jolted her back to reality as she exhaled, she refocused on the road in front of her, vowing to drive more cautiously from that point forward.

In order to find a spot, Eliza Rose navigated her automobile around the busy VCU parking lot while adjusting her spectacles. Her focus was quickly pulled to a couple in a passionate embrace inside a car amid the chaos.

The guy had wrapped his hand around the girl's beautiful platinum blonde hair. He put lips on her above her breasts while sporting an edgy black hairdo, evoking a gratifying response as her head dropped into the sofa. Even by the standards of today's society, Eliza couldn't help but find the entire scene to be somewhat out of the ordinary.

Eliza turned her head, a disgusted grimace on her face, and focused on the university building in front of her. She saw the girl smirk as she got out of the car and playfully grab the guy's neck before the momentary yellow tinge in her eyes vanished.

The couple's activities were briefly halted by Eliza's presence, and they turned to face her. She moved resolutely in the direction of the university entrance.

Eliza was okay with public demonstrations of affection as long as they stayed within specific bounds; holding hands and a little kiss on the lips were sweet gestures.

But what she had just seen was nothing less than an openly indecent display. She trembled with discomfort at the prospect of it.

Eliza knew she had already missed her first class of the day and that the next one wasn't due for another hour, so she made an appointment to see her counsellor.

Jared, her trusty buddy, jumped out of the car as she locked it, hurried towards the tree, and skillfully scaled it to find rest on a strong branch. He gave his head a careless scratch before falling asleep.

Eliza came into a bunch of sweaty young men playing basketball on her walk. They briefly turned to look at her as she passed.

One of the guys let out a snicker before making the provocative remark, "Could really use a maths tutor around here."

Another person joined in, "How about we all get some private lessons, honey?"

Someone threw the basketball towards the fence, hoping to get Eliza's attention. Eliza was unfazed because she was skilled at handling such situations and she decided to politely ignore their jeers. A few of the boys stole glances her way as they clustered around, murmuring between themselves, while others just laughed.

Eliza didn't think of herself as a people person, yet it looked like a lot of guys felt at ease talking to her. She couldn't help but observe that the majority of them looked very common.

She was aware that they were all on the same figurative ladder, attempting to advance their standing, and that sooner or later, she would run into them while making her own rise. They were also eager to go up the food chain. Sometimes a handsome person would flirt with her, but she could generally tell if it was real or simply a joke.

Eliza sped up and kept her look straight ahead, determined not to draw any more attention to herself. Unfortunately, she almost fell face-first as a result of her shoes slipping on the concrete path.

She quickly regained her equilibrium, took a deep breath, and kept walking while tightening the strap of her bag. Her palm became caught in the thick strands and she was unable to simply flip her hair.

Such was Eliza Rose's everyday existence.

CHAPTER TWO

S tacy, her face flushed with anger, stormed off down the hallway, with David in pursuit. The commotion attracted the attention of the onlookers, who turned to watch the unfolding scene.

"It's not about your stupid student ambassador duties, David. It's about our non-existent quality time," Stacy snapped.

Eliza, observing the scene, couldn't help but stifle a chuckle. Stacy's long hair swayed as she turned towards Eliza, while David shot her a glance with his piercing dark blue eyes. It seemed they had heard her slight amusement.

"I would watch it, freak," Stacy muttered before she walked away, leaving behind an awkward atmosphere.

Feeling self-conscious, Eliza bit her lip, hoping to avoid further attention. She wandered over to the student help desk, taking a deep breath as she patiently waited her turn to ask for assistance.

"Next!" the tired-looking lady behind the desk called out, her attention more focused on the computer screen than the students.

"I need directions to Student Services, please," Eliza spoke up, her voice soft.

The lady stopped chewing her gum and pointed in multiple directions. Impatiently, she interrupted Eliza, saying, "Turn left, then right, then left, then go straight." Irritated, she looked up at Eliza and barked, "Next!"

"Can you repeat that?" Eliza tried to ask.

"Turn left, then right... Just go straight and follow the signs," the lady snapped, already moving on to the next student.

Suddenly, a girl tapped Eliza on the shoulder. Eliza turned and flashed a grin, but the girl appeared frustrated, clearly not enjoying the long wait. "Excuse me, I'm kind of in a hurry. Are you done?"

The girl held out her palm and glanced back at the line of students, pursing her lips in impatience. Eliza apologized, "Uh, sorry," as the girl pushed past her to the counter.

Eventually, Eliza found her way to the counselor's office, a spacious area filled with chairs and tables. She approached the receptionist and joined the line to speak with someone. Above her, a sign displayed "Student Services" on a thick board.

"Excuse me, is this Admissions?" a voice interrupted her thoughts.

Eliza's gaze shifted downward, captivated by the guy's clean blue Vans. As her eyes traveled back up, she couldn't help but notice his rugged shorts and simple gray crewneck. She was momentarily speechless, lost in the depths of his light chocolate eyes. His long, mesmerizing eyelashes fluttered, hinting at a playful confidence as he subtly checked her out, causing a flutter in her stomach.

"N—no," Eliza stammered. "It's the Student Services Center."

"You're staring at me the same way you did earlier, Ms. Taylor Swift," he chuckled.

"Uh..."

Eliza could hardly believe that such a dry response was all she could muster. A guy was actually initiating a conversation with her, and all she could say was 'Uh'? She pressed her lips together, feeling a mix of embarrassment and excitement. Lost in her thoughts, she noticed the guy in front of her squinting, his hand casually resting on the strap over his shoulder.

"Ha ha, yeah, I like that song too," Eliza blurted out, unable to contain her enthusiasm. The words spilled out before she could even process them. She couldn't believe this was happening. The guy she never expected to see again was standing right in front of her, attending the same university. It felt as if her throat was closing up, her dorky side fully taking over as she struggled to find her cool composure.

Glancing behind him, Eliza caught sight of Stacy walking into her next class, her neck and chest covered in concealer, although the faint traces of hickeys were still visible. She couldn't help but cringe at the sight, a clear reminder of how different she was from the popular crowd.

"I mean—I like that song," Eliza corrected herself, her dorky nature momentarily taking over.

"Right, well, I'm Eric. Nice to meet you... uhm?" he introduced himself, his voice filled with genuine curiosity.

"E-lee-suh or Liza," Eliza replied, her cheeks flushing with a hint of shyness.

"Well, Liza, I'll see you later. I have to get to my next class. Just wanted to see if this was the right place," Eric said, his bright eyes shifting to the book he was holding.

A faint pout formed on his lips before he turned and started walking toward his class building, leaving Eliza standing there, her nerves tingling beneath her skin. She leaned against the doorway, watching him disappear down the hallway, her dorky heart racing with a mixture of excitement and uncertainty.

Lost in her own little world, Eliza didn't notice the door she was leaning against had a crack, and as she tried to push herself off it, her curly hair got caught in the crack. She let out a surprised yelp, causing some passing students to glance in her direction. Blushing furiously, she quickly untangled her hair and tried to play it off with an awkward smile, but deep down, she couldn't help but feel like the epitome of dorkiness.

Finally, she made her way to Mrs. Long's office, one of the counselors. An Asian lady, busy shuffling through paperwork and answering phone calls, caught sight of Eliza.

"Yes, uh huh, uh huh. Please hold," Mrs. Long spoke into the phone before picking it up again as it continued to ring.

"Graduation is on June seventeenth. You're welcome," Mrs. Long said into the phone.

"Mrs. Long," Eliza whispered, trying to get her attention. Mrs. Long waved her index finger and pointed towards the nearest chair, silently instructing Eliza to take a seat.

Eventually, the phones stopped ringing long enough for Mrs. Long to take a breather. She let out a sigh of relief and laid her head on her desk, feeling the weight of the day's tasks weighing on her.

"How can I help you today?" she mumbled, her voice muffled by the papers scattered on her desk.

"I wanted to check to see if I'm in all the right classes for this semester," Eliza said, her voice filled with uncertainty.

Mrs. Long turned to her computer and began typing quickly, her fingers flying across the keyboard. Eliza provided her ID number and answered the routine questions, her voice growing more animated with each response. Mrs. Long grabbed a clipboard and started scribbling down some notes.

"You need to take SDV," Mrs. Long informed her.

"SDV?" Eliza asked, puzzled.

"Yes, it's a student success class that focuses on time management and other important skills," Mrs. Long explained.

Eliza narrowed her eyes, a hint of annoyance in her voice. "I have to take it?"

"It's mandatory, and the only available slot is this Friday," Mrs. Long replied, her tone matter-of-fact.

Eliza studied the clipboard intently, her lips pursed in frustration. She glanced up at Mrs. Long and then back at the sheet of paper.

"Are you serious? That is so lame," Eliza muttered under her breath.

Mrs. Long handed her a pink slip with the directions and time for the SDV class. With a deep breath, she picked up the ringing phone once more, mustering her patience.

"This is Long. How can I assist you today?" she answered professionally.

Eliza closed the office door behind her, tucking the pink slip into her pocket. As she leaned against the door, she let out a frustrated sigh.

College life wasn't as exciting as she had imagined. People were often self-absorbed, walking out of classes without a care for anyone else. It felt like a chaotic ant colony, with students scurrying around, each defending their own little territory.

She dropped the papers she had been holding, her mind lost in her thoughts. They scattered across the glossy floor, and a few passing girls unknowingly stepped on them, leaving shoe prints in their wake. Eliza overheard one of the girls whisper to her friend, her words dripping with disdain.

"What a loser."

Eliza's heart sank. She was used to being on the receiving end of such comments. With her heightened hearing, she often caught snippets of conversations about her from a distance.

Gathering her registration papers, she stuffed them hastily into her purse. Just then, her best friend, Dawn, weaved her way through a group of jocks, her denim jacket and white high-waisted shorts making a fashion statement. The wind played with her recently dyed light pink hair, and her flawless skin shone under the school's lighting. Clutching her handbag, which proudly displayed the words 'Boys Stink,' Dawn approached Eliza.

"New bag?" Eliza teased, trying to lighten the mood.

"It was on sale at Hot Topic... I couldn't resist," Dawn confessed sheepishly.

"It's alright, Dawn. We all have our weaknesses. So, you already found a job? We just started the semester," Eliza said, falling into step with her friend.

"Yeah, can you believe it? I'll tell you all about it," Dawn replied, a mischievous smile playing on her lips.

Dawn glanced at Eliza's outfit, her expression shifting as she studied her curiously. With a slight motion of her finger, Dawn stopped Eliza from walking and crossed her arms.

"Dawn..."

"Nope, don't want to hear it. Twirl, missy, twirl," Dawn playfully instructed.

Eliza lowered her eyes, fiddling with her yellow cardigan, and kicked her feet around. Just earlier, the guys on the basketball team had catcalled her, but now she was receiving a compliment from Dawn. Today seemed to be going well for her.

"Thanks, I just threw it on. I was late today and missed class," Eliza explained.

"Overslept?" Dawn grinned.

"You know me so well."

"I'll buy you a dreamcatcher. They're on sale."

Eliza briefly remembered the nightmare she had earlier and considered telling Dawn about it. However, when Dawn nudged her with her shoulder, she decided against it. They continued walking, unintentionally stepping into an anthill.

It had been a lackluster first day of school. Eliza asked Dawn if she wanted to go to the mall, and Dawn agreed to text her once she got home.

Eliza deftly maneuvered through the rowdy students at school when she felt something furry bump against her ankles. It felt familiar. Closing her eyes briefly, she hoped that Jared, the cat, wasn't actually inside the school.

Opening her eyes, she found Jared walking next to her and immediately covered her mouth, glaring at him.

"You don't seem too excited to see me, Liz," Jared chuckled.

"Of course not! What are you doing in here?"

Everyone around them gave Eliza strange looks. From their perspective, she appeared to be talking to thin air. The students snickered and turned back to their conversations. Trying to act normal, Eliza headed toward the parking lot.

"Don't worry, they can't see me. I'm invisible to them," Jared reassured her.

"I don't care what you are! Get gone, Jare."

Eliza shooed him away, momentarily forgetting that there were people nearby. To them, it appeared as if she were talking to nothing but air. Placing her palm on her forehead, she noticed Stacy Meyer looking at her with a glare.

With a blink, Stacy disappeared. Eliza wondered if she had been hallucinating, but she could have sworn she saw a hint of yellow glimmering in Stacy's eyes.

If Stacy had noticed Eliza talking to nothing but air, she was likely to end up on her torture list. Eliza blamed the heat for getting to her head and shrugged off her awkwardness as she retrieved her keys from her purse and walked out of the school.

4

CHAPTER THREE

Eliza maneuvered her car into a tight parking spot outside her condo, her parallel parking skills falling short of perfection. She stepped out of the vehicle, taking a moment to survey her surroundings before making her way inside. As she entered the house, a distinct aroma invaded her senses, filling the air with the scent of burnt cooking.

In the kitchen, Eliza's mother stood over a pot, wrestling with a long, thick spaghetti noodle. With a swift motion, she placed the noodle on a plate before grasping the bunch in her hands and effortlessly snapping it in half.

The broken strands plopped into the boiling water, adapting to fit the constraints of the pot. Glancing up from her culinary task, Eliza's mother revealed her happiness through her brimming blue-grey eyes and flowing, wavy brown hair that cascaded over her shoulder. Her white, straight teeth formed a radiant smile as she looked up at Eliza.

"Hey, jellybean. How was your first day of adulthood?" her mother cheerfully greeted.

"I hate school," Eliza replied, her attention shifting to the noodles bubbling in the cauldron behind her mother. "Spaghetti?"

Dawn, Eliza's friend, descended the stairs from her room, playfully raising both eyebrows as she acknowledged Eliza's mother. "Isn't she just the greatest cook? Sorry, Liz, I forgot to text. I was shopping online."

"I wanted to surprise you! I got off work early, so, duh...had to see you guys' condo," Eliza's mother proudly proclaimed.

Eliza rolled her eyes, setting her purse down on the sleek granite table. "It's okay, Dawn. I'm happy to see you, Mom!" she mimicked her mother's infectious energy.

Her mother gracefully moved to the side of the kitchen, reaching for a nearby cookbook. Flipping through the pages, she soon located the desired recipe and emphatically pointed at the picture in the center.

"You..." Jared's voice rang out as he leaped through the kitchen window, having miraculously found his way back home. "I can't believe you left me at a place filled with disgusting humans. How could you do that to me? I will remember this forever." And with that, he swiftly darted away, disappearing deep into the confines of the condo.

"He'll get over it," Dawn nonchalantly remarked, her mouth full of a thick noodle.

"Eliza, really. How could you forget Jared at school? And no, it's not spaghetti. It's fettuccini, thank you very much," Eliza's mother corrected with pride.

"Mom, since when were you so interested in cooking?" Eliza muttered, making her way toward the kitchen table. She glanced at the cooking instructions. "You never cook. Let's just order Chinese food."

"It's a nice, warm welcome to your place! You two are grown women now. It's the least I can do."

Dawn was privy to Eliza's secret; she knew that Eliza was a witch. It was one of those secrets that couldn't be kept hidden from a friend who was always by her side. Moreover, Dawn's sharp intellect would have inevitably uncovered the truth about Eliza's magical abilities, even if Eliza hadn't revealed them herself.

Dawn was the only non-witch whom Jared allowed to see him. At first, Jared's frequent outbursts and flirtatious demeanor used to startle Dawn, but now she had grown accustomed to his mischievous ways.

Dawn's curiosity had always been a force to reckon with, often spiraling out of control. At this moment, her knowledge about Eliza was limited to the fact that she was a witch and possessed the ability to cast spells. Eliza, however, decided to keep it that way for now, realizing that she needed to learn more about being a witch before delving into discussions with Dawn.

Eliza's mother, on the other hand, had a habit of evading the topic of their kind. She would often claim that it gave her headaches, but Eliza suspected that there was another reason behind her reluctance to disclose more information about being a witch.

Eliza couldn't help but wonder what could possibly be more shocking than discovering she was a mystical witch. Lost in her thoughts, she picked up her mother's cooking book and idly flipped through its pages.

"If I leave this earth," her mother spoke with a tinge of sadness in her voice, "I want you to at least know how to cook a decent pasta." She quickly shook off the melancholy, her expression brightening. "So come over here and learn."

Her mother ran a finger through Eliza's hair, but predictably, it got tangled. She gently untangled her finger and raised an eyebrow, looking at Eliza expectantly.

"Please don't," Eliza pleaded. "And what do you mean by 'If I leave this earth'?"

Her mother's voice turned introspective as she mused, "Would you know where to go if I did?" She hummed softly while stirring the pasta.

Jared, the talking cat, hissed in warning from the kitchen table, suddenly becoming visible. "Grace..." he cautioned, a note of concern in his tone.

Grace watched him leap away, sighing in resignation. She turned her attention back to Eliza. "What are you talking about, Mom?"

"I'm just wondering," Grace replied, averting her gaze and muttering something under her breath.

"Miss Canary. You've told me a thousand times to go to her if anything happens to you."

"Just checking," Grace responded, her eyes conveying a warm smile.

She turned around, gathering ingredients, and leaned over the pot to sprinkle in some pepper before double-checking the book's instructions. Meanwhile, Dawn unpacked a few items from her boxes.

Their place wasn't particularly spacious, but the creamy light-colored walls lent a cozy ambiance to their humble condo. Despite its simplicity, it suited the two of them perfectly.

Dawn, who stood an inch or two taller than Eliza, had a passion for dancing and taught choreography classes for hip-hop and lyrical styles. They had been best friends since middle school.

"Damn it, I wasn't supposed to add that until step three," Grace muttered, her attention focused on the pot of pasta that had turned into a culinary disaster.

While Grace concentrated on rescuing the meal, Eliza strolled over to the island table in the kitchen. Pots and pans hung from hooks above the table, mainly serving as decorations.

"So yeah, Miss Rose. We were planning on getting Verizon to come over this weekend," Dawn's voice drifted into the kitchen as she conversed with Eliza's mother in the living room.

Eliza walked beneath the hooks, and her ears perked up at the clinking sound of pots hitting each other. The same sound reverberated around the kitchen, but this time, it grew louder.

Suddenly, two pots plummeted from their hooks, causing Eliza to let out a terrified shriek. She instinctively threw up her hands and closed her eyes, expecting the pots to crash onto the floor. Yet, to her surprise, a gentle force nudged her to the side, and a gust of wind brushed against her cheeks.

Opening her eyes, Eliza witnessed her mother deftly catching the falling pots before they hit the ground. Grace turned around, catching the other pot without even glancing. Her reflexes were astonishing, almost ninja-like. As she walked toward Eliza, her eyes appeared completely normal, devoid of any extraordinary glow.

"Are you okay?" she asked, concern evident in her voice.

"Y-yeah... I'm fine," Eliza stammered, still in awe of her mother's lightning-fast reaction.

Grace's gaze shifted to the hooks, her eyes narrowing. With a subtle intensity, she surveyed the kitchen, searching for something. Eliza couldn't fathom what she was looking for. Just a moment ago, her mother had been conversing with Dawn in the living room. How had she managed to reach Eliza's side so swiftly?

"How did you..." Eliza began, her voice filled with astonishment. "Your back was facing me. How could you have known?"

"Instinct," Grace replied, placing a hand on Eliza's cheek. "You're a witch, Eliza. Hence the talking cat over there." She pointed towards Jared, who was meticulously grooming himself. "It might be time for you to start trusting your instincts."

Eliza knew she was a witch, but her mother had never provided a thorough explanation. As far as she knew, they were the only witches on the East Coast. She had attempted countless times to fly on her broomstick, but it proved too small to lift her off the ground. It seemed utterly useless.

Eliza reminisced about the days when she would enter her closet and sing "Bibbidi Bobbidi Boo" from Cinderella, hoping for a magical transformation. Alas, nothing ever happened.

Apparently, Cinderella's fairy godmother was nothing more than a fictional character.

Lately, Eliza's ears had become attuned to sounds she never thought she could hear before. Despite wearing glasses, she found herself relying on them less frequently. Her vision had improved, and the need to squint had diminished.

When her mother had swiftly shielded her from the falling pans, she had attributed it to instinct. Could it be that instinct also played a role in her newfound clarity of sight? However, Eliza couldn't dismiss the fact that her mother often said peculiar things that bordered on the eccentric.

Adjusting her glasses, Eliza observed her mother's careful steps toward the pot she had been toiling over. The kitchen fell into an awkward silence. Dawn hurried in to check on Eliza, who assured her that she was unharmed before assisting with unpacking some of Dawn's belongings.

Grace's words echoed in Eliza's ears as she followed Jared upstairs, a sense of foreboding settling over her. Her grip tightened on her purse, the cool leather slipping against her sweaty palms. Thoughts of the hidden world Jared seemed to be a part of consumed her mind, leaving little room for anything else.

As she entered her room, she couldn't help but feel a sense of unease, like stepping into unfamiliar territory. Without much thought, she carelessly tossed her bag onto the bed, only to find Jared perched on the window counter, his presence immediately drawing her attention.

Eliza's gaze fell upon him, her eyes narrowing as she met his steady stare. She felt a surge of determination coursing through her veins, emboldening her to confront him. Her voice emerged, firm and resolute. "I know you know more, Jared. I know you're a witch too."

Jared leaned closer, stretching his back in a slow, deliberate motion. As he did, his feline features became more pronounced, his fur standing on end. His claws flexed, revealing their sharpness, a subtle display of power.

He yawned casually, a nonchalant façade masking any knowledge he might possess. The air around him crackled with an enigmatic energy. "Eliza, I know nothing," he replied, his voice laced with a hint of mystery.

"Sure you don't," Eliza retorted, her arms crossing over her chest. Frustration seeped into her voice, mixing with curiosity. "How come I can't cast spells or float in the air, like in the movies?" Her words were tinged with a hint of disappointment, a longing for the fantastical abilities often depicted on screens.

"Casting spells and floating? Really, Liza, you're hilarious," Jared chuckled, his tone dripping with sarcasm. "Witches are nothing like that. Calm your nerves." He licked his nose playfully, his eyes glinting mischievously. "In fact, they're mystical assassins, in charge of keeping what goes bump in the night, bumping...uh...elsewhere, unharming humans."

Eliza's mind raced, her thoughts connecting the dots and weaving a tapestry of understanding. She remembered the encounter she had with a mystic when she was younger, and the faint flickers of instinct that had begun to manifest within her. "Okay, I'm just not ready yet, it seems," she murmured, her voice tinged with a mix of acceptance and determination. Perhaps her inability to perform magic was linked to her broomstick malfunctioning. It all started to make sense.

Jared's purr rumbled in response, a comforting reassurance amidst the swirling uncertainties. "It'll come, don't stress it, Liza," he offered, his voice filled with a quiet confidence.

As Eliza's mind shifted gears, the urgency of her plans to go to the mall with Dawn suddenly flooded her thoughts. In a rush, she dropped the clothes she was holding and hurried downstairs, her footsteps resounding through the house like a marching drumbeat. She found her mother in the kitchen, gracefully slicing lettuce with fluid motions.

"Hey, Mom," Eliza greeted, a spark of excitement coursing through her veins, adding a lilt to her voice.

"What's up? I can hear it in your voice," Grace replied, her eyes betraying a tinge of disappointment, like the faintest flicker of a flame being extinguished.

"I kind of made plans with Dawn today. I was hoping we could do this big dinner some other time," Eliza explained, her words rushed and eager.

Grace halted her cutting, turning to face Eliza with a touch of sadness glimmering in her eyes. The knife in her hand seemed to pause mid-air, frozen in a moment of suspended anticipation. "I was thinking we'd spend some time together before you start your journey of college and, well, life," she said softly, her voice carrying a gentle weight.

"I know, but we'll always have time together," Eliza reassured, her hand finding its way to her mother's shoulder, offering a comforting touch.

Outside, the wind picked up, causing the leaves of the surrounding trees to rustle and collide, creating a melodic symphony of nature's chorus. Eliza's attention shifted to the plate her mother held, noticing a faint glow beneath her mother's sleeve. A flicker of curiosity sparked within her, prompting her to voice her observation. "Hey, when did you get more tattoos?" Eliza inquired, her voice carrying a hint of wonder.

Grace swiftly covered her arm, a hint of surprise crossing her features before she composed herself. Placing the plate on the table, she couldn't completely hide the glint of the mysterious markings beneath her sleeves. Urgently, she rushed into the bathroom, her voice trailing behind her. "You two have fun! Remember what I told you."

"I'm ready when you are, Liz!" Dawn's voice called from outside, breaking the brief, bittersweet moment between Eliza and her mother. Dawn twirled around in a circle, her laughter dancing in the air, before walking out of the house, ready for their outing.

As Eliza retrieved her bag from the couch, her attention was unexpectedly drawn to a glowing box on the coffee table. Before she could investigate further, Jared leaped in front of her, abruptly closing the box. Eliza's curiosity intensified, her eyes narrowing with suspicion. Her mother emerged from the bathroom, her sleeves rolled up, revealing glowing silver markings etched on her forearms.

"Oh, Eliza," her mother muttered, her gaze fixated on the front door, a hint of worry seeping into her voice. "I thought you were leaving with Dawn."

Eliza felt a pang of confusion at her mother's shock, her mind racing to grasp the sudden change in her mother's demeanor. It had only been a brief moment, a fleeting glimpse of something inexplicable.

Her mother hastily concealed her arms, but it was too late. Eliza had glimpsed the mysterious markings, their significance hovering on the edge of comprehension. Her mother's actions grew more frantic as Jared scratched the wood of the front door and made his way up the stairs, his necklace jingling with each step.

With a swift motion, her mother closed the kitchen curtains and turned to face Eliza, her finger tracing the markings on her arm with a mix of urgency and concern. "They know you're alive. We don't have time."

Eliza's confusion deepened, her brows furrowing in perplexity as she struggled to make sense of the cryptic words her mother uttered. Sensing the urgency in her mother's voice, she followed her lead, allowing herself to be guided into the living room.

The atmosphere was charged with an electric tension, thick with a sense of impending danger. Her mother's voice trembled as she spoke, her words rushing out in a desperate plea. "They're coming, Eliza. They're coming for us. We must be prepared."

Eliza's heart raced, her breath catching in her throat as her mother checked the locks on the front door and inspected the closed windows with a mix of determination and fear. Desperate for answers, she searched her mother's face, seeking solace and guidance amidst the rising chaos. Jared reappeared, carrying a clear bottle filled with black dust in his mouth. "What's that?" Eliza asked, her voice laced with apprehension, her eyes fixed on the mysterious substance.

Her mother crouched down, taking the bottle from Jared's mouth, her eyes locking onto Eliza's with a fierce intensity. "It's protective dust," she explained, her voice filled with a sense of urgency and resolve.

Without hesitation, grace shattered the bottle against the wall, causing Eliza's senses to heighten. The world around her seemed to slow, time stretching into an agonizingly suspended moment. The blood rushed through her veins like a raging river, the high-pitched ringing in her ears growing louder with each passing second. Overwhelmed by the sudden surge of sensations, she instinctively covered her ears, shutting her eyes tightly, seeking refuge from the impending storm of chaos.

The entrance of the condo emanated billowing, inky smoke, shrouding the doorway in an ominous haze that cast a foreboding shadow. Grace, her shoulder adorned by Jared, strode into the kitchen with resolute determination.

With practiced ease, she retrieved gleaming knives from the drawer, swung open cabinets, and procured crystal-clear bottles, their musical clinks echoing through the room as she slammed them down. Grace's unwavering focus then shifted to another cabinet, her hand reaching for the salt, tiny grains cascading into the awaiting vessels.

Eliza, sprinting to her mother's side, pleaded for answers amidst her desperation. "Someone please tell me what is going on!"

Grace, seemingly unperturbed by Eliza's presence, remained fixated on her task, her attention refusing to waver. She ignored Eliza's inquiries and continued her mission undeterred. Unyielding, Eliza snatched the bottles from her mother's grasp and pushed the salt bag across the counter, her voice laced with urgency. "What is that dark smoke, and why is it invading my home? I don't live with you anymore, so please mom, I don't want this witchcraft stuff in my life."

Eliza's gaze locked with Grace's, simmering with frustration. "Jared, prepare my broomstick," she commanded, prompting the feline to nimbly leap from her mother's shoulder and scurry into the living room. Eliza paid her mother's peculiar behavior little mind, dismissing it as another instance of her descent into madness, reminiscent of the time she had caught her conversing with herself in front of the bookcase.

Attempting to stow away a bottle, Eliza found herself blocked by her mother, and a struggle ensued as they grappled for control. Despite Grace managing to loosen Eliza's grip, it resulted in the bottle slipping from her daughter's fingers and shattering upon impact with the floor.

"Mom, seriously?" Eliza exclaimed, her exasperation evident as she attempted to push past the obstruction. Brushing her mother aside with an assertive arm, she forged ahead, resolute on proceeding unhindered. "Move out of my way."

"Eliza, put the bottles down," Grace interjected, swiftly snatching them away from her daughter. Suddenly, her movements froze, her senses heightened. Jared's ears perked up, and Grace instinctively took a step back, as if catching a distant sound.

"It's no one, Grace. We're safe," reassured Jared, his gaze shifting toward the dissipating cloud of black dust that invaded the house.

Eliza's frustration mounted as she demanded further explanations. "Tell me what is happening around here!"

Grace's voice dropped to a hushed tone, laden with caution. "If I divulge anything, they will discover your exact location. You've already seen the tattoos." Eliza glanced down at her mother's marked arms, a tangible reminder of the enigmatic world she had caught a glimpse of.

Jared leaped onto the kitchen counter, placing yet another bottle upon the table. "Listen to your mother. There are certain things that, as a witch, you are not yet ready to know." He appeared poised to reveal more, but a stern look from Grace silenced him.

"Don't utter their name," she warned, the gravity of her words resonating.

Eliza, bewildered by the cryptic conversation, interjected. "Who are you talking about?"

Grace met her daughter's gaze, her expression tinged with concern. "Listen, the protective dust wards off evil from this house, but your seeing my markings draws that evil in." She pursed her lips and placed her hands on Eliza's shoulders. "That's all I can tell you for now."

Jared hissed, rolling his eyes in frustration. "Well, we kind of, um... talked about them earlier, so maybe that's why you're feeling like this, Grace." Jared's ears folded, indicating his regret for delving into Eliza's curiosity about her instincts and the mystic encounter she had experienced when she was younger.

Eliza's lips parted, her voice wavering. "So, this is why you've been acting so peculiar..."

Grace eyed Jared and then shifted her gaze back to Eliza. "If you mention their name, it's like an alert for them. You're a witch, Eliza..." Her words trailed off, but Eliza interjected.

"And witches have responsibilities, right? But nothing has happened. Just calm down." Eliza looked at her mother with a mix of worry and frustration, grabbing her belongings. "You're seriously losing it, Mom."

Eliza knew that Grace despised being labeled as crazy. In the past, she had endured countless reprimands and punishments for such remarks. But Eliza was older now and wasn't prepared to deal with all of this at the moment.

Shooting her mother one last glare, Eliza swung her purse over her shoulder and made her way to the front door, swatting away the lingering tendrils of smoke that clung to her face. The doorbell chimed, and her mother rushed to answer it.

"This is my house, Mom. Let me handle the door."

"You're going out like that? Sweetheart, change your clothes," Grace insisted.

Eliza glanced down at her disheveled appearance, realizing she couldn't go shopping in her current state. Black dust marred her clothes, serving as a stark reminder of her mother's whimsical outbursts that had begun to wear thin. When she was younger, she dismissed them as a passing phase. Now, six years later, with nothing changed, her patience had worn thin.

"Forget the broomstick and all that. Be back before eight, or they'll come for me." Eliza lamented to herself. Her mother's imaginary friends were all she had left in that old house, the place she used to call home. She could accept the broomstick and the talking cat that wasn't really a cat but a magical familiar. What she struggled to grasp was the absence of magic itself.

Approaching the door to answer the insistent knocking, Eliza found herself shoved aside as her mother swiftly unlocked and swung open the door. A well-dressed man with dark hair stood on the steps, exuding an air of strength and confidence, his gaze fixed on Grace as she slipped out immediately.

"Hey, Liz! We don't have all day, you know," Dawn called out from outside.

"Yeah, sorry. Give me a second," Eliza replied, her annoyance seeping into her voice.

Hurriedly, she ascended the stairs, with Jared trailing close behind. "You need to talk some sense into my mother, Jared. I can't believe this..."

Jared nonchalantly plopped onto her bed. "Oh, hush. You should be used to it by now," he retorted, dismissively waving a paw in her direction. Eliza grabbed the scattered clothes strewn across the floor and trudged into the bathroom.

As she emerged, Eliza found Jared gone and an unsettling silence enveloping the house. Outside, Dawn murmured lyrics from her iPod, clutching her purse tightly. Eliza tightened her grip on her own purse and left the house, stealing one last glance at the new condo.

CHAPTER FOUR

D awn leaned against the side of Eliza's car, her gaze fixed on her phone screen as the daylight slowly waned, casting a dim glow over the surroundings.

They were parked near The Strip, a unique mall that differed from the conventional ones, with stores lined up along the street like an outlet. As the night approached, the sight of The Strip transformed into something truly captivating.

Beyond its assortment of stores, The Strip boasted a vibrant social scene, featuring clubs, pubs, and various other hangout spots. Dawn and Eliza strolled along the stone sidewalk, taking in the lively ambiance surrounding them.

Breaking the silence, Eliza voiced her thoughts, her words carrying a tinge of frustration. "I really need some stress relief today, especially after having to endure that tedious SDV class at school. Our mall is nothing like the typical ones, you know? It's like a whole experience, especially at night."

Dawn's attention momentarily shifted from Eliza's words as she became engrossed by a dress on display at Hot Topic. She turned her head back toward Eliza, her voice filled with awe. "You're considering trying out for the VCU cheer team?"

Eliza nodded, her eyes scanning the storefronts. "Yeah, it's something I've been thinking about. New school, new life, you know? I feel like I need to get involved in something."

Dawn smirked, her gaze returning to Eliza. "Come on, Liza. You're not invisible. Sure, you've got that wild, frizzy mane of hair," Dawn briefly glanced at Eliza's hair and then refocused on her face. "But seriously, you have friends. Like Jake, for instance."

A smile crept across Eliza's face as she considered Dawn's words, her mind dwelling on the possibilities that lay ahead.

Eliza's eyes rolled with annoyance as she recounted her past encounter with Jake. He had asked her to the homecoming dance during their freshman year of high school, but his clinginess and desire for a relationship had turned her off. The situation escalated, and he began stalking her throughout their high school years. Eliza had no interest in him now and didn't care to know his whereabouts.

Dawn's voice broke her reverie, "He's no one, Dawn. It's just you and me."

"And? What's the matter with keeping a small circle?" Dawn responded.

They both entered Urban Outfitters, greeted by a friendly associate. Dawn confidently replied, "Great," when asked how they were doing.

"Anything I can help you find?" the associate inquired.

"Nope, we're just browsing," Eliza said dismissively.

The associate, a short woman with caramel skin and a fashionable outfit, continued her duties, well-versed in the world of fashion. Eliza couldn't help but notice her expertise, attributing it to her job at the retail store.

As time passed, the friends had fun trying on clothes, playfully modeling for each other. Dawn confidently strutted out in tiger print joggers and bracelets, her pink hair adding flair to the ensemble.

Eliza emerged from her fitting room, sporting a black t-shirt with 'YOLO' emblazoned across it and a 'BARBIE' beanie. The irony of the hat choice amused her, leading to a genuine laugh.

Through the store's glass, Eliza spotted Eric outside, accompanied by a charming blonde guy. Her curiosity got the better of her, and she discreetly kept an eye on them, trying not to appear like a stalker.

Dawn interrupted her wandering thoughts, "Hey, Liz, I'll be in the fitting room. Gonna try this one," she said, sighing when she realized Eliza wasn't fully listening. "And...you're totally not listening to me. All right then."

Meanwhile, Eric and his friend exchanged words before glancing at the store where Eliza stood. Panicking, she quickly moved to another section of the store to avoid their attention. The motion sensor chimed as someone else entered the store, and Eliza took solace in the distraction, browsing through scarves and socks.

Suddenly, she felt hands around her waist, causing her to turn around and inadvertently press against someone's chest. To her surprise, it was Eric, who wore a mischievous grin.

Eric chuckled as he glanced at Eliza. "What are you wearing?"

Eliza smirked, teasingly asking, "You like it?"

"Love the beanie," he replied, flashing a smile. Gesturing toward the blonde guy next to him, he introduced, "This is my friend, Alex."

"Nice to meet you," Alex said, emanating the fresh scent of cologne with a hint of flowers, which prompted a quiet laugh from Eliza.

Curiosity piqued, she inquired, "So, what's up? Why are you on The Strip?"

Eric casually walked past an associate named Dawn, with whom they had a previous encounter. Dawn smiled at him before wandering off into the men's section of the store. Meanwhile, Alex decided to explore the store on his own.

"Nothing much. I just heard about The Strip on Tumblr and wanted to check it out. We don't have this kind of stuff in Canada," Eric replied.

Eliza considered inviting them to join her group but hesitated. As the words were about to escape her lips, something seemed to trouble her, and she hurried back to the fitting room to check the time on her phone.

Seeing that it was 9:00 p.m., she felt a pang of concern. Her mother and Jared had warned her countless times not to be out past eight, citing vague reasons related to her safety. Their concern for her wellbeing was evident, and she knew it was essential to abide by their wishes.

Dawn emerged from the fitting rooms, accidentally dropping some clothes. Alex promptly rushed over to assist her. As he helped her pick up the items, Dawn's eyes locked with his, and a grateful smile spread across her face. Alex leaned casually against a fixture while they engaged in conversation, his mannerisms suggesting a hint of flirtation.

Eliza observed their interaction from a distance, contemplating whether to intervene or not. She didn't want to disrupt whatever was brewing between Dawn and Alex, especially considering her mother's peculiar beliefs about witchcraft and the impending departure the next day.

Sidling up to Dawn, Eliza whispered, "It's nine o'clock."

Dawn was engrossed in conversation with Alex, who seemed to be quite taken with her, engaging in playful banter. Her laughter filled the air, drawing attention from Eliza, who observed the scene with narrowed eyes. It appeared as if Dawn was oblivious to everything around her, her focus solely on Alex.

"Really, cats are amazing. I have, like, five," Dawn confidently declared, playfully showing five fingers. Alex wrapped his arm around her waist as they strolled toward the fitting rooms, his hand enveloping her smaller fingers amidst the shelves of beanies and socks. It was as if Eliza had become invisible, an unnoticed observer in their presence.

Eliza couldn't help but feel uneasy about their behavior. She wasn't an expert on retail policies, but she was pretty sure that opposite genders weren't supposed to be in the fitting room together.

Curiosity got the better of Eliza, and she followed them discreetly. As she neared the fitting room, Dawn's giggles faded away, replaced by an odd sense of discomfort.

Peering around the corner, Eliza was surprised to witness Alex and Dawn locked in a passionate embrace in front of the large mirror. This was uncharacteristic of her friend.

Dawn seemed entranced, as if under some spell. She spoke incoherently, her words blending with the kisses. It was apparent that she wasn't entirely comfortable with this public display of affection, yet she allowed it to continue. Eliza couldn't help but wonder why she was behaving this way, especially with someone she had just met.

Alex's intense gaze met Eliza's as she quietly approached them. She hesitated for a moment, then gently whispered, "Dawn, we should probably get going. Jared will be waiting for us."

However, Dawn remained captivated by Alex, seemingly lost in the moment. He ignored Eliza's presence, focusing solely on her friend. He touched her cheek and hand, and then began to caress her under the ribcage. Eliza could sense that Dawn was uncomfortable, and she knew this wasn't the type of affection her friend would willingly embrace.

Conflicted and concerned, Eliza wondered what could be compelling Dawn to act this way with a relative stranger. She wished to protect her friend from any discomfort or harm, but she also knew that it wasn't her place to intervene forcefully. She could only hope that Dawn would soon regain her senses and recognize what was truly best for her.

In the bustling department store, Eliza's voice echoed with authority, cutting through the air like a blade. "Hey! Get off of her, creep," she shouted, her hands forcefully pushing the guy against one of the glossy fitting room doors.

Her body surged with adrenaline, her brows furrowing with an intense anger that she struggled to contain. She clenched her fists, envisioning herself dragging him across the ground and delivering punishing blows. With pursed lips, she strode purposefully toward the guy.

His eyes widened in shock, but a smirk played on his lips, as if he found the situation amusing. Undeterred, Eliza seized the collar of his shirt, pulling him closer before delivering a swift punch to his face.

Without a second thought, her knee shot out, jabbing him in the stomach, sending him sprawling to the ground. His hand instinctively went to the side of his jaw, his smirk replaced with a look of disbelief, his eyes locked onto Eliza's.

Dawn, who had been in a trance-like state, seemed to snap out of it at the sound of Eliza's actions. Her eyes grew wide with shock as she saw Eliza by her side, a glimmer of recognition in her gaze. The commotion had brought her back to reality, and she coughed, holding her hand against her throat.

Meanwhile, the guy struggled to regain his composure, wiping blood from his lips with his thumb. He staggered to his feet and hastily made his way out of the fitting room, retreating from the confrontation.

Eliza turned her attention back to Dawn, concern etched on her face. She gently moved her friend's hair away from her face and noticed a fading colorful glitter on her lips, triggering a sense of familiarity within her.

"Are you okay, Dawn?" Eliza asked, her voice softening as she assessed her friend's condition.

Dawn appeared disoriented and bewildered. "I'm so confused. I was—I was just looking at this purse," she stuttered, her voice fading. "I—I don't remember anything else." She shook her head, attempting to make sense of the situation. "Who was that guy? What the hell?" She rubbed her mouth in disgust.

Eliza sighed, trying to find the right words. "You were talking to him, and things got a bit... intense between you two." She cast a glance around the store, only to notice the guy had already left. "Well, he's gone now."

Dawn looked at Eliza, her expression a mix of confusion and disbelief. Her hand went to her lips, as if searching for answers she couldn't grasp.

Eliza's voice trembled slightly as she spoke, "I don't know. The guy you were talking to, Eric's friend..." Her eyebrows furrowed, indicating her concern about the situation. "We need to go. It's nine."

As Eliza entered the open fitting room, she felt a sense of relief taking off the clothes she had tried on. Time had slipped away, and she had spent longer in there than intended. Emerging from the fitting room, she noticed Eric's watchful gaze fixed on her. She walked over to him while her friend Dawn settled her purchases at the register.

"Sorry, I have to go. Family problems at home," Eliza explained, casually flicking her hair behind her shoulder.

"Oh, curfew? No need to lie," Eric joked, his hands in his pockets.

"No, really. I just have to go."

Eric's expression turned puzzled, and he set down the clothes he had been considering purchasing. He raised an eyebrow and watched as Eliza lifted her hand to check her breath.

"Are you going to keep running from me every time we meet up somewhere?" he asked, gripping her arm tightly, causing her to flinch from the pain.

"Hey, that hurts." Eliza looked up at him, her eyebrows knit together in discomfort.

"I'm playing with you, Liza. Calm down." He smirked, then waved goodbye as he left the store.

Eliza couldn't shake off the odd feeling of being grabbed like that. She rubbed her arm and realized there was a bruise where he had held her.

After leaving the store, Eliza and Dawn strolled down the strip, the golden white glow of streetlights and neon lights from bars and clubs illuminating their path. They encountered a few drunk individuals stumbling around, their laughter echoing through the night.

"Hey, babe, you lookin' sexy," a guy called out to Dawn, who pretended to be engrossed in texting to avoid confrontation.

"You lookin' sexy," Eliza teased, playfully nudging her friend.

"Shut up."

Their destination, Eliza's car, was a few blocks away, situated near a peculiar French jewelry store. The walk seemed to stretch on forever, and Eliza's legs grew heavier with each step, her muscles aching from a day of standing.

"So, who was that guy you were flirting with at Urban Outfitters?" Dawn inquired.

"Oh, I met him on the way to school. He noticed me embarrass myself while I was driving. I was dancing to Taylor Swift, and he watched," Eliza said with a faint smile. "I also ran into him again that same day on the way to student services. His name's Eric." She brushed her frizzy hair from her face and glanced toward the ground, lost in her thoughts.

"You like him..." Dawn teased, a mischievous glint in her eyes.

Eliza's words caught in her throat as she struggled to form a coherent response. "Wha—"

"Don't even start, Liza," Dawn interrupted, her laughter bubbling up.

"I don't—" Eliza began, but her protest was swiftly cut off by her best friend.

"I'm your best friend. Shut up," Dawn said, her laughter mingling with her words.

As the words hung in the air, Eliza couldn't help but wonder if her feelings for him were so transparent. After all, they had only just met, and she couldn't be sure if she truly liked him or if it was just a passing interest. The guy was peculiar, grabbing her as if it were a joke and leaving a bruise behind.

Attempting to ease the tension, Eliza spoke up, her voice tinged with uncertainty. "I'm sure he doesn't know anyone since he's from... you know, Canada and all."

"Oh... and you know where he's from? You go, Ms. Eliza Rose," Dawn playfully smacked her friend's shoulder.

They continued walking, the neon lights gradually fading, leaving the surroundings dimly lit with only the streetlights casting a glow on the sidewalk. Across the street, a dark path loomed, littered with discarded garbage cans. Eliza rummaged through her purse, shaking it in search of her keys, the jingle of metal eluding her. Dawn, lost in her music, hummed along to the lyrics, her headphones firmly in place.

A soda can rolled onto the street, propelled as if deliberately kicked.

A shiver ran down Eliza's spine as an eerie sensation gripped her stomach. Slowly, she raised her gaze, scanning the darkness to discern the source of the sound. Finding nothing but obscurity, she hastened her search for the keys, her fingers finally closing around them just as footsteps echoed from the dark path, crunching on loose gravel.

Moving toward her car, Eliza pointed her key's remote, causing it to emit a confirming beep, unlocking the vehicle. "Hey," Alex's voice reached Dawn, devoid of any warmth. She paused her singing, removing her headphones. The intensity of his gaze mirrored the one he had given her in the fitting room earlier.

A smile tugged at the corners of Dawn's lips. "You look familiar."

"Yeah, we should get going, Dawn," Eliza interjected, her voice betraying a hint of unease. She cleared her throat, attempting to redirect her friend's attention. Alex maintained his gaze on Dawn, his smirk hinting at hidden intentions. Adjusting his hair, he bit down on his bottom lip.

Without a sound, he turned on his heels and disappeared into the dark path. Unthinkingly, Dawn followed suit, skipping after him.

Thickening blood coursed through Eliza's veins, her heart racing with trepidation. Her trembling hands clutched her keys, mirroring the tremors within her. Searching her surroundings, she sought the presence of any bystanders who could assist her if needed.

Alone on the desolate street, Eliza couldn't help but feel as if she were stranded in an unfamiliar void.

"Dawn!" Eliza's voice echoed through the narrow path as she hurriedly chased after her friend. Panic consumed her, causing her breath to quicken and the frigid air to sting her lungs, making each inhale a struggle.

In the enveloping darkness, Eliza's senses heightened. She stumbled over discarded trash, the sound of her steps merging with the sudden appearance of a black cat colliding with a nearby trash can. Seeking solace, she pressed herself against the rocky wall, stifling the urge to scream. The narrowness of the path amplified her claustrophobia, overwhelming her thoughts.

Carefully, Eliza continued onward, her voice subdued as she abandoned calling out for Dawn. In the pitch-black darkness, her lack of glasses left her completely blind, and she berated herself for forgetting them at home.

A memory resurfaced, her mother's voice echoing, mentioning something about instinct. She couldn't shake off Jared's accusatory voice, proclaiming her to be a witch.

Taking a deep breath, Eliza strained her ears to catch any sound, and faintly, amidst the eerie silence, she heard giggles. Dawn's giggles. Determination surged within her, fueled by the knowledge of Dawn's location.

Her newfound agility surged through her limbs as she sprinted, drawing upon her mother's reflexes. Almost as if channeling her, Eliza glided swiftly toward the sound of Dawn's laughter, determined to rescue her from this unknown threat.

Her speed increased, causing her hair to whip back from the gust of wind, striking her face with force. Ahead, a faint light illuminated the dead end, suggesting that Dawn and her captor were somewhere within its glow.

Eliza strained her eyes to see through the dimness, her heart pounding in her chest. As she approached, the figures became clearer. Dawn's voice, heavy with intoxication, welcomed her.

Golden sparkles of blue and green dust adorned Dawn's skin, while Alex, his actions almost vampiric, showered her with kisses, leaving behind a trail of glitter. His wings, sharp and ethereal, fluttered gracefully upon his back as he hovered slightly above Dawn, his touch venturing beneath her clothing.

The tattoos that wrapped around Alex's smooth skin formed intricate swirls, his pointy ears protruding from beneath dark green attire. Eliza couldn't help but notice the change in his hair, once blonde, now a luminous dark grey, illuminated by his fluttering wings. The breeze they created caressed her face, carrying a soothing fragrance of fresh lilies and roses that invaded her nostrils.

As Eliza's vision blurred, her nose twitched in response. She recognized this scenario, but the memory eluded her grasp. Determined to intervene, she discreetly scanned the ground, hoping the enigmatic creature wouldn't notice. His attention remained captivated by Dawn's allure.

With a tremor of fear, Eliza discovered her broomstick hidden in her pocket, her grip tightening around its rusty handle, the rough metal scraping her palm. Overwhelmed, she steadied her trembling hands, taking a deep breath to regain composure.

"Let her go!" Eliza's voice reverberated through the air, charging forward towards the disturbing tableau. Waving her useless weapon aimlessly, she hoped to deter the creature. Yet, despite her desperate actions, nothing changed. Frustration gripped her as she pressed the button on the broomstick, but it remained inert.

The creature abruptly ceased his advances on Dawn, turning his attention towards Eliza. Glitter glistened on Dawn's lips, and drool trickled down her neck, her face etched with a dazed smile, reminiscent of their encounter in the Urban Outfitters fitting rooms.

Eliza knew she must have appeared quite peculiar, carrying her broomstick everywhere she went. As she wandered along, a strange creature suddenly swooped toward her. Reacting quickly, Eliza deftly dodged to the left, bracing herself against the nearby wall.

Her eyes caught sight of a discarded trash can lid lying on the ground. "This might actually be more useful than the broomstick," she thought to herself. But her focus returned to the creature, which was now fixated on Dawn, holding her tightly by the neck. Without a moment's hesitation, Eliza grabbed the lid and hurled it with all her strength at the creature's head.

The impact of her strike jolted the creature out of its trance, releasing its grip on Dawn, who fell to the ground, laughing with relief. The creature, still recovering, stumbled backward, shooting a furious glare at Eliza. Its eyes, resembling shimmering crystals, locked onto her, and it revealed its sharp teeth by pulling back its red lips.

Intriguingly, the creature had an array of rainbow-colored tattoos that began to glow. Despite its monstrous appearance, there were still traces of its original human features. Eliza found herself simultaneously terrified and captivated by this creature's beauty.

Suddenly, the creature lifted off the ground, soaring menacingly toward Eliza. It gripped her neck with icy cold hands, causing her to gasp for air as its colorful wings stirred a gust of wind against her face.

Struggling to breathe, Eliza felt her vision starting to blur. Her heart raced, and in a desperate attempt to break free, she clawed at the creature's hands, trying to pry them away from her throat. But the creature maintained its grip, chuckling as it cracked its neck to the side.

Just when it seemed all hope was lost, Eliza heard a loud thud nearby. Blinking through tears, she managed to focus on the source of the commotion. Someone was coming to her aid.

The approaching person's footsteps quickened, and Eliza could hear the sound of gravel crunching under their boots. Determined to survive, she mustered her strength, planting her hands firmly on the ground, and prepared to take action.

Soon, a figure with colorful, silver lights darted past her, flipping gracefully in front of the creature. With a swift motion, the person activated a slender object, turning it into a medium-sized bar that they skillfully twirled in the air. Eliza's eyes remained fixed on this new savior.

Stopping the twirling, the person pressed a button on the bar, and two daggers sprang forth from each end. The imposing figure now stood before the creature, clad in a striking black suit adorned with studs, leather pants, and heels.

The creature's rainbow markings seemed to crawl over its face as it focused on its new adversary. Its eyes continued to shift between various colors as it took to the air again, its wings flapping wildly.

Swift as the wind, the lady sidestepped the creature's attack, allowing her to swipe at its right wing. A mist of rainbow colors rose from the wing as it vanished into thin air. With a crash, the creature plummeted to the ground, sending gravel flying in all directions.

Eliza wasted no time and quickly moved to the side, seeking shelter by the nearby wall, grateful for the arrival of this enigmatic woman who had come to her rescue.

Eliza's eyes widened as she watched the mysterious woman approach Alex with an air of confidence. Her face was partially obscured, but her glowing silver markings were unmistakable, leaving no doubt that she was a witch.

Swiftly, the woman reached out, seizing Alex by the neck and forcefully pulling him away from Eliza. Alex hissed and retaliated, attempting to kick her, but she displayed an impressive agility, evading his attack effortlessly.

The woman wielded an unusual weapon—a broomstick adorned with silver lines. As she skillfully maneuvered it, she landed a precise strike on Alex's cheek, leaving a visible gash. Eliza squinted, trying to comprehend the weapon's properties; it was clear to her that the broomstick was more than just a simple cleaning tool.

The creature's markings glowed even brighter, and he tried to retaliate, swinging his fist towards the woman. But she effortlessly dodged his blow, countering with a swift kick that sent him stumbling backward, crashing into a nearby wall.

With a fluid motion, the witch closed the distance between them once more, jabbing the end of her broomstick under his right nipple, causing a spray of rainbow mist to erupt from the wound.

Eliza couldn't believe what she was witnessing—the broomstick seemed to be infused with some kind of mystical power. The woman continued her assault, inflicting another painful puncture under his left nipple, eliciting an agonizing sound of bones cracking.

As the creature writhed in pain, the woman's attention turned to Eliza, addressing her as her daughter. Eliza was stunned by this revelation, but there was no time to process it as the woman resumed her attack, kneeing Alex and slamming his head against the wall.

The white cat that had been observing from the stairs now approached, its movements elegant and mesmerizing. Unfazed by the situation, it observed the scene, tail swaying gently. The woman's boots crunched against the gravel as she turned to face Eliza, her hair whipping in the air. Her gaze held a mixture of intensity and mystery.

"Who's the crazy witch now?" Grace uttered, leaving Eliza speechless, struggling to comprehend the reality of the situation and the witch being no one other than her mother.

CHAPTER FIVE

Eliza's eyes widened in disbelief as she witnessed the astounding display of power. Grace, the woman she had known as her mother, had swiftly and effortlessly defeated the creature that had posed a threat to their lives.

Grace's movements were fluid and precise, lacking any trace of hesitation as she plunged a weapon into the creature's chest. It was a sight that shattered Eliza's perception of her mother, revealing a skilled and ruthless assassin.

With a cold gaze, Grace glanced down at Eliza before turning away, leaving her behind. Jared, Eliza's companion, voiced his disapproval, his words laced with concern.

"And you wonder why we constantly remind you to be home before eight," Jared remarked.

Wiping wet glitter off her jacket, Grace muttered under her breath, "Fairy blood is the worst."

Locking her eyes on Eliza, Grace ordered, "Get up, Liza."

Shaking off the pain from her fall, Eliza gathered herself and pushed aside her confusion. She hurriedly followed her mother, her mind racing with questions. Could her broomstick, the innocent object she had always known, truly transform into a deadly weapon?

Perhaps her mother's seriousness about her carrying it at all times and adhering to curfew had a valid reason.

Yet, the woman walking ahead of Eliza seemed distant and foreign, a fearless warrior devoid of mercy or emotion. It contrasted sharply with the nervous and solitary figure Eliza knew at home, talking to imaginary things late at night.

Eliza's friend, Dawn, slumped against the rocky wall, her head resting wearily. She appeared to be asleep, her chest rising and falling in a slow rhythm. Eliza moved to assist her, but her mother swiftly intervened, striking her hand with leather gloves.

"Are you insane?" Grace snapped. "Can't you see the glowing marks on her neck and skin?"

Taking a closer look, Eliza noticed an array of colorful marks, resembling hickies, illuminating Dawn's skin. Dawn's fingers twitched involuntarily.

"Fairy hickies are contagious, Eliza," Grace explained, annoyance seeping into her voice. "The toxic saliva from those marks enters the bloodstream, amplifying emotions and numbing reactions. The victim becomes trapped in a seductive trance until death or corruption takes hold."

Adjusting her gloves and securing her chocolate brown hair in a ponytail. Grace could see the memory replaying in her Eliza's eyes. The pain, the burning arm, it all came rushing back. Grace averted her gaze, refusing to meet Eliza's questioning stare, and refocused on Dawn.

"You should be grateful you didn't succumb. I suspected something like this might happen during your transformation," Grace muttered in disappointment. "You should never be alone out here without me. I told you to be home before eight."

Jared chimed in, emphasizing the importance of Eliza's mother's warnings. "We both warned you."

Unable to contain her frustration any longer, Eliza yelled at her mother, her voice filled with anger and desperation. "You never tell me the truth about who I am! Maybe, just once, you could be honest with me!"

Forcing herself away from the scene, Eliza trudged down the path towards her car, determined to distance herself from the chaotic revelations. In the distance, she could hear Jared's voice.

"Are you going to cure her here or back at Eliza's place?" Jared said.

A sudden surge of energy crackled through the air, accompanied by a gust of wind that blew Eliza's hair into her face. Startled, she turned around, only to find Jared and Dawn nowhere in sight.

Eliza's hands trembled uncontrollably as her heart raced in her chest. She hurried towards her car in a desperate attempt to escape the overwhelming events of the night. However, her frustration grew when the car wouldn't open, and she struck the door in anger, recoiling in pain from the impact.

In the midst of her emotional turmoil, Grace, Eliza's mother, appeared, clad in a hooded jacket and black leather pants, illuminated by the moon's soft glow. She sensed her daughter's vulnerability and urged her to toughen up, demanding the car keys.

With a shaky hand, Eliza reached for her purse lying on the ground and handed it to Grace. Grace quickly located the keys and ordered Eliza to get in the car. Anxious about her friend Dawn's safety, Eliza inquired about her whereabouts.

"Don't worry, she's safe at your place," Grace reassured her.

Upon returning to her condo, Eliza was surprised to find Dawn already there, the evidence of the earlier encounter with a fairy still visible on her skin in the form of hickies, emitting a faint glow. Grace smoothly approached Dawn and administered a silver glowing syringe to her neck, injecting her with a shimmering liquid. As a result, the hickies faded away, and Dawn's twitching ceased.

Drained and overwhelmed, Eliza stumbled into her bedroom, collapsing face-first onto her bed. Her loyal companion, Jared, joined her on the foot of the bed, expressing concern about her actions.

"You're in trouble," Jared nagged.

"Please, not now, Jared. I can't handle anything else," Eliza muffled her response through her bed sheets.

Jared persisted, questioning Eliza's decision to confront a fairy.

"It had my friend. That thing definitely wasn't Tinkerbell," Eliza muttered, frustrated with the situation.

"Wake up and pay attention to what's going on around you," Jared advised, trying to steer her towards a more prudent path.

Eliza lay sprawled across her bed, replaying the night's events in her mind as she exhaled a heavy sigh. Her laughter from earlier echoed, the sarcastic tone still lingering in the air.

"So you knew about my mom being some badass, sexy ninja monster killer too?" she had said with a smirk. "What else is there that I don't know already?"

Jared's response was serious, trying to dissuade her from making light of the situation. "Eliza, this isn't a time for you to be making bad jokes."

Undeterred, Eliza snapped back at him, her sarcasm biting. "Shut up, you thing! What are you? A devilish cat that can talk?" Her mind drifted to memories of her mother's heroic acts and how she had been saved by her when she was younger, feeling a strange sense of déjà vu.

Jared mumbled something under his breath before abruptly leaping out of the open window into the night, leaving Eliza behind.

Lying on her bed, Eliza let out a sigh, her mind troubled by the night's revelations. The memory of her mother's voice echoed in her head, speaking about a transformation and the dangers of fairy hickies.

She thought about her mother's broomstick and the magical things it could do, realizing why her mom had been so cautious whenever she didn't have it around. Eliza had the broomstick with her, but it didn't respond like her mother's; it remained dull and unresponsive.

Frustration and confusion mingled as she retrieved the broomstick from her purse, glaring at it with hope for a miraculous change. But it remained stubbornly ordinary, failing to transform into the deadly weapon her mother's could become.

As if on cue, Jared slipped back into the room through the window, returning from wherever he had gone.

"Become a deadly weapon!" Eliza shouted at the unyielding broomstick, giving it a desperate hit.

Jared's mocking voice chimed in, "It's not going to do anything with you yelling at it. Your transformation isn't done yet."

Transformation? The word brought back memories of her mother's cryptic words back on the dark path.

"What transformation?" Eliza demanded, her curiosity and fear growing.

Jared hesitated, clearly torn between the desire to protect her and the need to share information. After glancing nervously at the door, he leaned in and whispered, "It's like a puberty but for witches, clearly your transformation hasn't started yet, which is why your broomstick isn't working."

Eliza nodded and said, "okay what else can you tell me?"

Eliza nodded, her eyes eager for more information. "Okay, what else can you tell me?" she asked.

Jared, her feline familiar, licked his paw before delving into the valuable knowledge Eliza sought. "That creature in the alley is called a mystic, and the more you know, the more likely they are to seek you out. But clearly, you don't care about that," he snapped, glancing anxiously at the door. "In order to use the broomstick for protection, the transformation itself has to run its course on you. The only real way to defend yourself from these mystical creatures is through physical fighting, though that has proven to be a failure for past witches."

His beady eyes darted behind Eliza towards the door.

"So that's why everyone's been keeping it hush hush around here. Well, hell, did you guys expect me to just sit around looking for answers?" Eliza grumbled.

"Would you shut up?" Jared paced along the windowsill. "Your eyesight is affected because you're in the middle of the transformation. It'll get better, just like your hearing did. And, we love you..." Jared hesitated as if he needed to cough up a furball. "But seriously, as your familiar, I'm supposed to guide and protect you. That's why I'm telling you to chill for a bit and let the transformation process do its thing."

Eliza realized that her recent vision problems were likely connected to the ongoing transformation. She recalled her mother taking her to the doctor for glasses without mentioning the true reason behind her vision issues. Her agile movements while running down the dark path and avoiding trash cans suddenly made sense, given the changes she was undergoing.

"Basically, I'm becoming like a ki—" Eliza began.

The door to her room swung open, and her mother entered, her gaze shifting between Eliza and Jared.

"I would love some cat food right now," Jared muttered, clearing his throat as he swiftly passed Eliza's mother. He glided through her legs and darted down the stairs.

Eliza's mother squinted at the departing familiar before turning her attention back to her daughter, her hands on her hips. "Why didn't you use your broomstick to protect yourself?"

"Like I know how to use it."

"It should've come naturally to you. It's instinctual. Oh, you're probably still in your transformation," her mother realized, understanding that Eliza was a late bloomer.

With a huff, her mother spun around and left the room. "You should be following," she called back.

Eliza got up on her toes and followed her mother in a military-style stride. They entered the living room, still filled with unpacked boxes. Eliza's gaze fixed on one of the boxes on the floor, and she mumbled to herself as her hand hovered over one of the books.

As Eliza entered the living room, her eyes immediately fell upon an ancient book Grace had pulled out. Grace blew away the thick layer of dust, revealing a silver and dark purple cover, adorned with the same silver lines that Eliza recognized from her own broomstick. Despite its age, the pages were surprisingly pristine, as if the book were brand new. Her heart skipped a beat—this was the very book she had seen on her home bookshelf.

Grace settled on the couch, crossing her legs, and patted the seat next to her, inviting Eliza to join. Intrigued, Eliza couldn't resist asking, "What's that?"

With a hint of pride, Grace replied, "Well, it's a grimoire, of course. When you get a chance, I would like for you to read this. I have to go. I'm meeting another witch tonight to control some mystics that have created a mess, and I'm a few hours away. Please don't get yourself caught up like you did tonight."

Eliza pondered for a moment, suspecting that Grace was probably meeting the man she had mentioned earlier. She wondered why Grace hadn't told her about him yet. As Eliza opened the grimoire and flipped through its pages, Grace let out a deep sigh and placed it in her lap.

"Don't worry about Dawn. She won't remember anything that happened tonight," Grace reassured.

"Why is that?" Eliza inquired.

"I fixed her memory with my syringe. It's sort of like a broomstick, but you can only get one at certain places, like Witcher's Place, a store for witches," Grace explained.

As Grace prepared to leave, she reminded Eliza, "I love you, and remember, I'm only a few hours away." She then called out to Jare, asking him to take care of her daughter before heading out.

As Eliza watched her mother leave, memories from her childhood flooded her mind. She rubbed her forehead, trying to gather her thoughts. Suddenly, there was a knock on the front door, but before Eliza could answer, her mother quickly stepped ahead of her and opened the door. Giving Eliza a last glance and a wave, she headed out.

Jared, the family companion, approached, bouncing into the living room and leaping onto the arm of the chair. He flipped through the pages of the grimoire with his paw, stopping at a picture of a fierce-looking teenage girl with silver tattoos and a broomstick. She was Eliza's great grandmother, Mellissa Morolov, a powerful witch.

Jared turned to another page titled "Mystics" under the subtitle "Magical Creatures." Eliza's heart raced with both excitement and trepidation. Finally, she could understand what her mother had been murmuring about to herself. As she thought about the fairy her mom had fought, she felt a shiver down her spine. Jared sensed her unease and offered his support.

"I'm supposed to be helping you with all of this stuff. You're different than other witches. I know this is all new to you. I just hope you can grasp it, okay?" Jared said.

"I'm getting there, Jare."

Jared went on to explain the mystical creatures to watch out for, particularly fairies, elves, and mermaids. With her transformation beginning, they would sense her presence. He advised her to avoid reacting to any strange events at school and to keep herself out of the crowd.

Eliza muttered, "Not like I get attention anyway," as she looked down at the grimoire, knowing that her journey into the world of magic was just beginning.

Eliza's mind drifted back to the earlier encounter with her mom, a memory etched vividly in her thoughts. She recalled the way her mom's face contorted with concern and a hint of fear when she spotted Eliza's witch markings earlier that day.

Without uttering a word, her mother's actions spoke volumes, giving Eliza a glimpse of the hidden meaning behind the concealed tattoos. Though she couldn't fully grasp the connection between the marks and her mom's witch abilities, Eliza understood why her mother had kept them secret, protecting her from a world she didn't fully comprehend. Not a single tattoo adorned Eliza's own skin.

Turning her attention to Jared, Eliza addressed her curiosity. "I know this is the book you leaped on to keep me from seeing it a while ago." She glanced at him, seeking answers. "Why are you guys telling me everything now?"

"Mystics are going to come after you no matter what, Eliza. They're blended in amongst many normal people here in this world." His eyes lingered on the book, as if it held untold secrets. "You just have to know how to prepare yourself for them. We were trying to protect you, but clearly that didn't work when you were younger, and I think it just made your mom and I a bit paranoid it would happen again."

Eliza's heart pounded in her chest as fragmented memories resurfaced, revealing a truth she had long suspected but never fully acknowledged. Fourteen years old, a fateful encounter with a fairy had changed everything. Her mom's possible tampering with her memories became a haunting possibility she couldn't ignore any longer.

In waves, the forgotten events rushed back, like a river breaking through a dam. Regret washed over her, knowing that those lost memories might have held the key to understanding Jared and her mother, two people who had always seemed distant and enigmatic. If only she had realized it sooner, perhaps she could have connected with them on a deeper level.

Guilt weighed heavily upon her conscience, pressing down like a dark cloud above her. The ignorance she had displayed, the times she had misjudged their actions or words, now gnawed at her soul. She wished she had been more compassionate, more understanding, and less quick to judge.

In this moment of realization, Eliza couldn't help but feel a profound sense of responsibility. As the memories unfolded, she understood that her actions had consequences beyond her own experiences. There were connections she had missed, emotions she had brushed aside, and pain she had overlooked.

Now, armed with the truth, Eliza was determined to make amends. She vowed to seek out Jared and Grace, to apologize for her ignorance and attempt to bridge the gaps she had unknowingly created. This journey of introspection and reconciliation would be her way of honoring the lost time and the feelings she had failed to comprehend.

As the weight of her past lifted, a newfound determination filled her heart. Eliza knew that embracing the truth was the first step in healing old wounds and building stronger connections with those around her. And so, with a sense of purpose, she embarked on a path of self-discovery and redemption, knowing that the road ahead might be challenging but necessary for her growth.

With the book in her hands, Eliza contemplated the things she already knew about herself and the mystic world that lay in wait. First and foremost, she was a witch, but she didn't rely on spells; instead, her broomstick had become a formidable weapon.

Secondly, her mom possessed an extraordinary blend of witchcraft and ninja-like abilities, and their adversaries were the enigmatic mystics. The image of the eerie fairy she had witnessed lingered, leaving her imagination to conjure even more unsettling creatures that witches confronted.

Her thoughts turned inward as she confronted her own transformation - a "second puberty" for witches. The feeling of excitement mixed with terror swirled within her, uncertainty shrouding what this metamorphosis would entail. Her mom's actions during the recent mystic encounter hinted that she might be undergoing a metamorphosis of her own, a transition into becoming a mystical assassin like her mother.

Eliza mused on the misconceptions about fairies, now shattered by her recent encounter. Unlike the benign Tinkerbell of folklore, these fairies bore sharp and fearsome wings, harboring malevolence beneath their ethereal beauty. Their lethal kiss served as a stark reminder of the dangers she now faced.

CHAPTER SIX

T he crisp, warm wind blew the pages of Eliza's psychology book around as she placed the palm of her hand in the middle of the crease. She crossed her legs on the bench where she was sitting. Today was club day, and a bunch of students from different organizations were standing outside, advertising how cool their clubs were.

"Join our dance team! We teach hip-hop and other styles!" a girl called out, waving a bunch of freshmen to her stand. A mixture of guys and girls danced to the music blasting from the boom boxes, drawing a crowd around them who began to clap in rhythm.

Noticing Dawn running towards the crowd and disappearing into the midst of it, Eliza closed her book, surprised that Dawn would just run into the throng like that. But then again, dancing was her thing. Curiosity got the better of her, and she decided to walk over to see what was going on.

As Eliza approached, there was a roar of applause. Dawn's hips swayed slowly from right to left, ending with a sharp hip tick as she rolled her body to the center. She crisscrossed her legs and gracefully circled in place, captivating the onlookers. Dawn clapped with the crowd to pump them up as she executed a series of different formations around a guy, showcasing her impressive dance skills.

Eliza watched in awe as Dawn danced gracefully, the cheers of the crowd surrounding them. "Go Dawn!" she thought, even though her friend couldn't hear the words of encouragement.

With each beat colliding, Dawn's lips pursed in determination as she placed her index finger on the guy's chest, guiding him through the dance. Then, in one swift move, she executed a flawless round-off flip, drawing gasps of amazement from the onlookers.

The energy was contagious, and students rushed over to sign up for the dance club, led by the confident figure in the hot pink crop top and high-waisted white shorts, standing tall on a picnic table. Eliza couldn't help but smile, thrilled for Dawn's success.

In the midst of the excitement, a light poke on her back made Eliza turn around, finding Eric standing there, his eyes locked onto hers. "Isn't that your friend?" he asked, genuinely curious.

"Yeah, that's Dawn. She's incredible," Eliza replied, feeling a sense of pride in her friend's talents.

"I can see that. Can you dance like her?" Eric inquired, a playful glint in his eyes.

Eliza shrugged, blushing slightly. "Nah, dancing isn't really my thing," she admitted, feeling a little self-conscious.

Eric's grin widened, and he ran a hand through his brown hair. "Well, what about raving? Jumping around and having fun?" he suggested, his gaze warm and inviting.

Eliza chuckled, appreciating his easygoing nature. "Yeah, I do enjoy having a good time, but Dawn's the real dancer," she said, her eyes returning to her friend's captivating performance.

As the crowd started to disperse, Eliza realized she needed to catch up with Dawn. But before she could move, Eric gently held her back, his touch surprisingly gentle.

"Hey, you and this grabbing thing needs to stop," Eliza teased, looking up at him.

Eric's expression softened, and he spoke with sincerity, "I just don't want you to go. What if I want you to stay?"

Eliza felt her heart skip a beat, a warm smile spreading across her face. "You could've just asked," she said softly, the unspoken connection between them growing stronger as they shared a moment of understanding.

"Would you stay?" Eric flirted, his playful tone lingering in the air.

Eliza chuckled to herself and began walking toward the building for her SDV class. She noticed Eric following her out of the corner of her eye.

"So what? You're a stalker too?" Eliza teased, looking over at him. "You can say that."

Eliza pressed on, curious. "No, really?"

"Calm down. I'm just playing with you, Liza," he replied casually. "It's E-lee-suh."

"Sorry. I'm heading to my SDV class too. I think it's this way," Eric said, walking alongside her.

As they walked, Eliza couldn't help but notice the significant height difference between them. She felt her face turn red with embarrassment, realizing that Eric was already being quite forward with her, despite them being nothing more than acquaintances at this point. She wanted to resist being drawn to him, but she couldn't deny that he had a certain charm and attractiveness that occasionally got to her.

Taking a deep breath, Eliza's enhanced hearing picked up on some whispers from a few girls nearby.

"David's missed school for a week," one girl muttered to another.

David? The guy dating Stacy?

Remembering what Jared had advised her to do - to stay out of the crowd - Eliza decided to heed his words for once. As she continued walking, the girls ahead of her kept muttering and gossiping. She noticed a piece of white paper stuck in one of the girl's hair and shook her head in disbelief as the girl squirmed around.

☆☆☆

"Calm down. Let me get it out," one of the girl's friends offered, attempting to fix her hair. "It wouldn't be so bad if you went to a salon once in a while."

Eliza waved off the offer with a smile. "Continue with the story. I'll fix my hair later."

"That's Stacy Meyer's boyfriend. Skipping school doesn't sound ethical to me," her friend whispered.

"What does it matter to you? We don't even know the guy," the girl said, her curiosity piqued.

"I saw him with another girl yesterday on the strip," her friend shared.

"Oh, awkward. Time for the slut to get cheated on for once," the girl remarked with a giggle as they continued walking down the hallway.

☆☆☆

Just then, Eric tapped Eliza's shoulder, pulling her out of the conversation and back to reality. She looked up at him and responded, "Right. Well, uhm, cool. I'll see you in class."

With her cell phone in hand, Eliza continued down the hallway, making her way toward SDV class. As Eliza weaved through the bustling hallway, someone carelessly bumped into her, sending her belongings flying in all directions.

Ugh, seriously, today was just not her day. But then, like a hero, Eric swooped in to help, picking up her scattered papers with a charming smile that made her heart skip a beat.

The guy who had bumped into her had the audacity to return, trying to act all apologetic. But Eric wasn't having it. He stood up, jaw clenched, and confronted the guy, ready to defend Eliza like a knight in shining armor.

"What's up?" the guy challenged, his bravado showing cracks in the face of Eric's intensity. "Do you have something to say?"

Eric took a deep breath, trying to keep his cool. "You bumped into her, man. Look at the mess she has to clean up," he retorted, his voice firm and unwavering.

Eliza felt a mix of emotions wash over her. It was kind of over-whelming how protective Eric was being, but at the same time, she appreciated his support. Her heart raced, unsure of what would happen next, as she covered her mouth in shock.

The guy glanced at Eliza for a moment, then shifted his gaze back to Eric. "She was in my way. I was just trying to help," he muttered, his bravado fading as he felt the weight of Eric's stare.

The tension in the hallway was palpable, and everyone seemed to hold their breath, waiting to see how things would play out. Eliza's heart pounded as she watched the exchange unfold, her mind racing with conflicting thoughts and emotions.

In an instant, Eric threw a punch, catching the guy off guard. Gasps and whispers rippled through the crowd as Eliza's eyes widened with surprise. She couldn't believe her friend had just thrown a punch, but she also couldn't deny the rush of adrenaline she felt.

He shouted, "You're really going to stand here and lie to my face?" His eyes focused, and anger emanated from him. Eliza stood up, rushing to intervene before Eric hit the guy again, but he gently moved her out of the way to deliver a kick. "Watch where you're going next time, dipshit!"

As the situation settled, Eliza offered her help to the guy, expressing her concern. "Are you okay? I'm sorry about—"

The guy looked up at her and said, "Don't worry about it," before coughing and placing a hand over his stomach as he walked away.

"What a joke," Eric chuckled, but there was still a hint of tension in his voice. "If she wasn't here, I would've knocked your face out!" he yelled at the retreating guy.

Eliza's heart was racing, and she felt torn by the situation. "You didn't have to start a fight over it. Really, something is wrong with you," she retorted, her voice a mix of concern and frustration.

Eliza adjusted her purse's strap over her shoulder, trying to shake off the intense emotions from the hallway encounter. Why did people have to get so worked up over trivial stuff? It was just a few papers, for crying out loud. But as she walked, Eric caught up to her, surprising her with his sudden appearance.

"I care," he said earnestly, causing Eliza to look at him, taken aback by his genuine concern. It was as if he could read her thoughts. He quickly added, "I care about you, and anyone who disrespects you disrespects me. We're trying to be friends here, and I'm not about to let that go because of some idiot."

Eliza wasn't sure how to react to Eric's protective side. They were still getting to know each other, and she didn't want to jump into anything too quickly. Trying to lighten the mood, she brushed off his words and playfully retorted, "Wow, you're pretty intense for a new friend. But okay, point taken."

With a small smile, she walked into their SDV class, feeling a mix of emotions swirling inside her. Eric followed, and as they entered, Mr. Drude, their teacher, was slouching at his desk, his belly peeking out from tight pants. Eric and Eliza found their seats, becoming the last students to arrive.

Mr. Drude stood up, his hands clasped together, and locked the door, sending a signal that this would be a serious class. Eliza settled into her desk, readying herself for what she expected to be a long and possibly challenging session.

Across from her, Stacy Meyer oozed confidence, her platinum blonde hair perfectly styled. Eliza couldn't help but admire Stacy's self-assurance. She seemed to know exactly who she was, and it made Eliza reflect on her own journey of self-discovery and navigating new friendships.

Stacy glanced at Eliza and then at Eric as he walked past her. In a split second, she flipped her hair back and strategically positioned her body to follow Eric to his seat. With a calculated move, she lowered her shirt, showing as much cleavage as possible. Her eyes fluttered in Eric's direction as he settled into his seat. Eric, feeling the weight of Stacy's gaze, awkwardly looked at Eliza for a moment. Eliza, trying to hide her amusement, shrugged her shoulders in response.

"Welcome to hell," Mr. Drude clapped his hands together, creating a thunderous sound that instantly grabbed the attention of the students. They stopped whatever they were doing to watch him.

Stacy was the last to turn around, casually checking her cuticles while the rest of the class focused on Mr. Drude.

"Do not talk to me, do not talk to others, do not move, do not breathe, and do not sleep!" Mr. Drude yelled, his voice filled with frustration. "Simple."

With that, their teacher sat back in his chair, tossing his feet over the desk, and slowly dozed off. Eliza couldn't believe it. This was supposed to be a class about success tips for college, and it felt utterly useless. She wasn't even getting any credit for it. And now, all their teacher planned to do was sleep?

Eliza sighed inwardly, feeling exasperated. "Kill me now," she muttered under her breath, sharing a knowing look with some of her classmates who felt the same way. This was going to be a long and unproductive class, and she couldn't wait for it to be over.

Eliza gazed out of the window beside her, watching as little droplets of rain started forming on the clear glass outside. She absentmindedly brushed her fingers across the cold surface, lost in her thoughts. Hours seemed to pass by, and eventually, her head was buried in her arms on her desk, feeling the weight of boredom in the monotonous class.

Suddenly, she felt a poke on her back, followed by a light splat noise from underneath her desk. Turning around, she found Eric grinning mischievously at her. She mouthed, "What?"

He pointed at the floor in front of her, drawing her attention to a crumpled piece of white paper lying there. It became clear that he had playfully thrown it her way.

Suppressing a laugh, Eliza bit her lip and extended her foot to drag the crumpled paper within her reach, nearly losing her balance in the process. She carefully unfolded it and discovered girly hand-writing inside.

It amused her, and she chuckled to herself, quickly covering her mouth to stifle the sound. She glanced up at Mr. Drude, the teacher, to make sure he hadn't noticed. It was hard to tell if he was even awake; the class seemed to be as uneventful to him as it was to Eliza.

Feeling assured that she hadn't drawn any unwanted attention, Eliza turned her focus back to the paper. With Eric nearby, there was no telling what kind of mischief he had written on it. But curiosity got the best of her, and she began reading what the paper held in store.

Addicxion with me? Tomorrow?

-Eric

Before Eliza could write back, Stacy shot her an irritated look, and then, with a smirk directed at Eric, she grabbed some paper from her folder and tore it into tiny pieces. Without any warning, she sprinkled the torn paper all over herself and on the floor, creating a mess. Eliza watched in confusion, wondering why Stacy would do something like that.

"What the heck, Eliza!" Stacy snarled, waving her arms around, feigning distress. Ah, that's why she did it. Mr. Drude, who had been dozing off, suddenly woke up, almost falling out of his seat. He quickly adjusted his glasses and scanned the classroom, his eyes settling on Stacy.

"Mr. Drude, look what she did! She threw all of this on me!" Stacy pointed directly at Eliza. "Call campus security!"

Eliza's heart raced as she realized what was happening. It was a setup, and Stacy was trying to blame her for the mess she had created. Feeling a mix of frustration and anxiety, Eliza couldn't believe Stacy's audacity.

"Eliza! Stay after class with me," Mr. Drude shouted, clearly unhappy with the situation.

Eliza snapped at the ridiculous accusation, and Eric's mouth dropped in disbelief. He couldn't believe someone would believe such a false claim.

As soon as the class ended, students began to leave. Stacy, with a smirk of satisfaction, was the first to get up, reveling in the success of her devious plan. Eliza rummaged through her purse, placing the papers she had been doodling on inside it.

"I told you to watch it, freak," Stacy taunted.

Eliza followed Stacy with her eyes as she left the classroom. Meanwhile, Mr. Drude, the teacher, instructed Eliza to stay behind to clean up the mess Stacy had purposely made. It annoyed her that Stacy seemed to get away with causing trouble.

After tossing the shredded papers into the trashcan, Eliza left the classroom with a sigh of relief. Once outside, she noticed Eric leaning against a wall nearby, arms crossed in front of him.

"Took you long enough," Eric joked. "What's that girl's problem?"

"I have no idea." Eliza replied, clutching her purse as they headed outside toward the parking lot.

"So, Addicxion? With me?" Eric asked.

"What exactly is that?"

"It's a rave, like a party."

As Eric's invitation lingered in the air, Eliza's nerves began to dance inside her. She brushed the strands of her thick hair out of her face, unsure of how to respond. Part of her was excited by the prospect of going out with him, but another part hesitated due to his anger problems, which had caused some concern.

Carefully looking down at him, Eliza mustered the courage to respond, her voice slightly shaky, "Sure, I'll go." She started to walk away, but then hesitated, turning around to add, "Only if Dawn comes with."

To her surprise, Eric pumped his fist in the air, confirming, "She's already planning on going."

Dawn? Eliza couldn't help but wonder when her friend had developed an interest in the rave scene. She had always thought Dawn was more into hip-hop clubs and such. The fact that Dawn hadn't mentioned her plans to Eliza hurt her feelings a little, but she tried to shrug it off, not wanting to dwell on it.

Before any further thoughts could consume her, Eric interrupted her thoughts. "Okay, I'll see you then."

"Right," Eliza replied, her mind still buzzing with a mix of excitement and uncertainty about the upcoming outing. As she continued on her way, she couldn't help but wonder how the night would unfold, hoping it would be an adventure worth remembering.

After the intense moment, Eric quickly hopped on his motorcycle, revved the engine, and zoomed out of the school parking lot, leaving a trail of excitement behind. Skidding onto the road, he disappeared from sight in no time, leaving Eliza to process the event that had just unfolded.

Eliza watched Eric's departure, a mix of emotions swirling inside her. Despite the unexpected punch, she couldn't help but admit that there was something intriguing about him. "Guess he isn't that bad," she mused quietly to herself, the memory of his protective gesture lingering in her mind.

With a soft smile playing on her lips, Eliza shook off the lingering tension and got into her car. Her heart felt a flutter of excitement, and she couldn't deny the hope that maybe, just maybe, Eric had a softer side beneath his tough exterior.

"Well, at least I hope he isn't," she whispered to herself as she started the engine, ready to drive away.

CHAPTER SEVEN

T he front door creaked open, and Eliza stepped into her house, her backpack slipping from her shoulder to the floor with a soft thud. Her heart seemed to skip a beat as her eyes fell upon the scene before her—Dawn, nestled on the couch with a guy perched on top of her. Flustered, Eliza instinctively shut the door behind her and hurried toward the refuge of the kitchen.

"Who was that?" The guy's voice was hushed, the urgency clear.

Dawn, her cheeks flushed, extricated herself from the couch and hastily ran her fingers through her hair. With a sense of urgency, she followed Eliza into the kitchen, where Eliza pretended to be engrossed in inspecting the contents of the fridge. She was hoping to sidestep the impending awkwardness that was rapidly approaching.

"Eliza! You're back sooner than expected," Dawn's voice carried a tinge of mortification as she covered her mouth.

"My teacher let us out early due to the storm," Eliza muttered, her face partially hidden by the open freezer door.

Spying what she was after, she retrieved the carton of ice cream and placed it on the table. From the corner of her eye, she noticed a shirtless guy in black basketball shorts ascending the staircase, his gaze briefly flitting between Dawn and herself. Dawn, clad in an oversized grey sweater that likely belonged to her companion, attempted to conceal her discomfort behind a forced grin.

"Looks like someone's having quite the time," Eliza remarked, her tone laced with a hint of playful sarcasm.

Dawn's hand swiftly scooped up a discarded shirt from the floor before she sauntered into the living room, the fabric dangling from her grip. "He's just a friend," she declared, her tone casual but carrying a hint of defensiveness.

"With benefits," Eliza couldn't resist interjecting, her words accompanied by an arch of her eyebrow.

Dawn's response was to rush upstairs, her room's door clicking shut in her wake. Amused, Eliza let out a soft chuckle as she observed the scene. From a window, Jared nimbly leapt onto the table, his feline gaze locked onto her, particularly on the cookie she was munching.

In a swift motion, he dashed to her side, his teeth clamping onto the treat still in her hand. A bemused shake of her head was her only reaction, a smile tugging at the corners of her lips. Who would have thought she'd be going to a rave?

Gently scooping Jared into her arms, Eliza twirled him around the room in an impromptu dance. Amidst their playful movements, she held up one of Jared's paws as if they were sharing a secret.

"Alright, this—" Jared began, cutting her off with her antics. " Eliza... This is... Inapropi—" his words were disrupted and speech disjointed by the motion.

Eliza's hair flowed like a silken waterfall over her shoulder as she flicked it with an air of nonchalance. Jared's protests were momentarily silenced as she playfully tossed him onto her bed, the rebound sending him momentarily airborne.

Swiftly, Jared dug his claws into the sheets, his fur bristling with a hint of anxiety. He released an exasperated sigh. "Good lord."

Her gaze lingered on her reflection in the mirror, the sight igniting her dance once more. A flutter of disbelief and excitement coursed through her veins as she contemplated the night ahead.

She reveled in the thought that, even if it wasn't an explicit date, someone beyond Dawn wanted to spend time with her. The flutter of butterflies took residence in her stomach, a reminder that tonight held the promise of something new and unexpected.

The door to the room emitted a soft creak, and Eliza's attention shifted from her phone to the doorway. Dawn stood there, arms crossed and a mischievous glint dancing in her eyes. A slight grin played upon her lips as she observed her friend.

Without hesitation, Eliza flicked her phone behind her and flopped onto her bed, kicking her legs into the air in pure excitement. Dawn strolled over to the radio, her fingers silencing the strains of Katy Perry's song that had been filling the room.

"So, did he ask you?" Dawn's words were loaded with curiosity.

Eliza blinked, caught off guard. "What do you mean?"

A knowing smirk danced across Dawn's lips. "I mean, did my little matchmaking scheme actually work?" She arched an eyebrow, awaiting Eliza's response.

Eliza's realization hit her like a ton of bricks, and in her mock frustration, she grabbed a pillow and hurled it toward Dawn's face. Quick as a cat, Dawn deflected the incoming missile and playfully dove onto the bed beside her friend.

"I swear, Dawn, one day you're going to get it from me," Eliza mock-threatened, though a glint of amusement lingered in her eyes.

Dawn's grin remained unapologetic. "Oh, come on, Eliza. It's not like you were planning on making the first move. And remember your whole 'new school, new location, new life' mantra?"

Beside them, Jared leapt onto the bed, his presence a reminder of the ongoing conversation. "What about staying out of the crowd?" he interjected, a tinge of curiosity coloring his words.

Eliza glanced at her feline companion, then back at Dawn. "Why should I avoid the crowd?" she questioned, more to herself than anyone else. "Maybe it's time to step in and see what life has to offer."

A quick glance in Jared's direction and Eliza's resolve strengthened. "I promise, I'll steer clear of the crowd. And yes, I'll even bring my trusty broomstick."

"Always bring the broomstick," Jared chimed in, his tone strict and matter-of-fact.

Eliza nodded, her lips curving into a determined smile. "And this time, I'll actually use it."

A sense of newfound conviction filled her, even though the reality was she didn't quite know how to work the broomstick's magic.

"Alright then. Have a blast," Jared said, already bounding downstairs.

An unrestrained squeal escaped Eliza as she flung herself at Dawn, engulfing her in a hug. Dawn looked up from her thumb-twiddling, a curious smile on her lips. "I was just talking to some friends about the party, and he kind of just jumped into the conversation," she began, her eyes dancing with mischief. "I happened to slip your name in there, but I swear I didn't drop a hint about you tagging along."

Eliza's eyebrows lifted, intrigued. "So..."

Dawn leaned in with a grin. "It was all him, but I'm dubbing it the unintentional setup I didn't intend to set up. And, girl, he's not just fine, he's fire. Why say no to that? Besides, a bit of buff dude action never hurt anyone!"

Eliza instinctively covered her mouth, a mix of astonishment and, truth be told, a little dread. The idea of "buff dude action" with Eric was slightly overwhelming. The guy had been displaying weirdly protective tendencies despite them knowing each other for only a couple of days.

Dawn's voice snapped her back to reality. "Listen, it's going down at Virginia Beach, alright? We need to leave early 'cause that place isn't just around the corner. Let's aim for around two," she said, her words rushing out before she took a breath. Then, her expression shifted. "Oh, your rave outfit! I totally spaced on that. I need to shoo Brandon out first."

Eliza arched an eyebrow, intrigued. "Brandon, the guy occupying your room?" She laughed, brushing her hair from her face. "Alright, spill the tea."

"Oh, there was this dance battle on campus. I ended up going head-to-head with him, and it turned into this whole big thing. Seriously, so much fun!" Dawn's voice was animated as she recounted her story. "Were you around during club day?"

"Yeah, I was there, but I kept my distance. Was definitely rooting for you though," Eliza replied, a hint of warmth in her tone.

Eliza raised an eyebrow playfully. "You and him seem to be moving at quite the pace, huh?"

Dawn couldn't help but giggle, her cheeks turning a faint shade of pink. "Well, he's cute. The way he talks to me is just... ravishing. It's weird to admit, but there's a wicked charm about him."

With a toss of her vibrant pink hair, Dawn exited the room, leaving Eliza to her thoughts. As she pondered what she had just heard, Eliza couldn't shake off the unease that the term "wicked" carried.

Considering her newfound connection with mystics and the potential dangers that came with it, being associated with anything "wicked" felt far from comforting. She couldn't help but think that maybe carrying a knife for self-defense wasn't such a terrible idea after all.

Minutes passed by, and Dawn didn't return to Eliza's room to sort out the details of their plan for getting her rave outfit. The house was steeped in an unusual quietness, the persistent rain outside drumming relentlessly on the roof.

Eliza's gaze wandered to the window, where a woman in a nearby house caught her attention. The lady was engrossed in arranging her flower pots, her gaze lifting to briefly meet Eliza's before returning to her task.

Concerned, Eliza left her room and headed towards Dawn's. The door was a statement in itself, adorned with stickers of punk rock bands that she knew Dawn adored. After a quick knock, she rapped her palm against the wood about five times, her curiosity pushing her actions.

A pungent odor wafted out from under the door, so strong that Eliza instinctively covered her nose with her hand. As the door slowly creaked open, the scent grew even more overpowering.

The scene that met her eyes caused her heart to thump wildly in her chest. A creature, fur-covered with peculiar long hind legs and a hunched back, loomed over Dawn, casting ominous shadows across her room.

Fear was evident in Dawn's eyes, her mouth silenced by some unseen force, the creature's viscous drool glistening just above her belly button. Eliza's eyes locked onto Dawn's, the silent plea in her friend's gaze sending a chill down her spine.

Abruptly, the creature shifted its focus to Eliza, its unsettling red eyes locking onto her. A sharp snout jutted from its face, and a shiver ran down Eliza's spine as she involuntarily took a step back, her body meeting the wall. A gasp escaped her lips as the creature charged toward her, its intent clear.

Eliza staggered back, managing to escape from Dawn's room. Her feet carried her swiftly downstairs, the creature's growls echoing in her ears, a chorus of menace. But fear gripped her so fiercely that she stumbled and lost her footing on the steep staircase, her descent a whirlwind of terror.

Amid the chaos, Jared appeared, his usually cheerful tail now held low. Eliza's voice trembled as she tried to warn him. "J-Jared, go upstairs..." Her words faltered as the creature seized the back of her shirt, its strength propelling her against the wall with a brutal force.

"The innocence in this house..." The creature's gravelly voice sent shivers through Eliza, its words striking a chord of foreboding deep within her.

Eliza's mind raced, trying to grapple with the unthinkable truth. The creature that had masqueraded as Brandon was no ordinary threat – it was a mystic, a shapeshifter. Dread coiled tightly around her as the creature moved closer, its claws leaving sinister marks on the walls. The chill in its voice was unmistakable. "So, you're the new witch making waves around here?"

Glancing around for help, Eliza spotted Jared darting into the kitchen. Panic surged within her – why was he leaving her now, when she needed him the most? She edged away from the creature, her heart pounding with a desperate plea for escape. Its menacing grin sent shivers down her spine, its sharp teeth gleaming in the dim light.

"To think I was going to end Dawn's life, but I find myself craving yours," the creature hissed, a predatory hunger in its eyes.

Before she could react, the creature lunged, and in that heart-stopping moment, hope seemed lost. But then, like a burst of courage, Jared sprang into action. Armed with a knife, he leaped onto the creature, driving the blade into its neck. A whirlwind of chaos ensued, with the creature writhing in pain beneath Jared's assault.

"Eliza, finish it!" Jared's voice urged her, a mixture of desperation and determination.

Summoning her resolve, Eliza gripped the knife, her trembling hands finding strength. With a swift kick, she toppled the creature onto its back, its eyes locking onto hers in a final, malicious gaze. As the blade descended, mingling screams filled the room, a chilling symphony of demise.

"End it – take off its head!" Jared's voice guided her, relentless in its urgency.

The blade connected again, slicing through flesh and bone, sending a shudder through Eliza. And then, a rush of wind brushed past her, and as her eyes flicked open, the creature was gone – as if it had never existed.

"That was..." Eliza began, her voice quivering, grappling for words to encapsulate the enormity of the experience.

"Freakin' badass," Dawn's voice chimed in, a mixture of astonishment and admiration. She leaned against the wall, her eyes wide, chest rising and falling with the rush of emotions.

Eliza straightened, her gaze locked on her friend, a mix of shock and disbelief dancing in her eyes. "Dawn, it was a mystic – a shifter."

""Oh my God, I had a feeling something was off with him. He had this weird aura, and he was so insistent about going down to the second stage so early," Dawn exclaimed, her eyes widening as the realization hit her. She recoiled, recognizing the dangerous path she had almost treaded. "Oh my God, that's like... bestiality territory." We both cringed, repelled by the disturbing thoughts our minds had entertained.

My grip on the knife faltered, and it dropped to the ground with a clatter. Dawn was still visibly shaken, her breaths coming in uneven bursts. She pressed her back against the wall, her hand instinctively fixing her hair in a nervous gesture. Her gaze flickered toward the discarded knife, and as I moved closer, she raised her hand, a silent plea for space.

"I'm sorry, just... don't come closer right now. I need to gather myself," she managed to utter, her hand rising to cover her mouth as if to steady herself. "I-I can't even wrap my head around this, Eliza."

"Dawn, remember that Eliza is a witch, and mystics are drawn to human innocence," Jared's voice cut in, a trace of annoyance in his tone.

Dawn's eyes darted to him. "But aren't witches innocent?"

"Some are. But with Eliza undergoing a transformation, her innocence is like a beacon, which is why I'm concerned about her going to the party alone," Jared explained, his expression reflecting his unease.

My heart sank as I absorbed his words. The world of mystics and witches was becoming more intricate and dangerous with each revelation, and it seemed that innocence was a currency that carried immense power.

Eliza's hands settled on her hips, her eyebrow arching with a mixture of skepticism and curiosity that played out on her features. "Hold on a second, what's this talk about innocence?" She shifted her gaze to Dawn, a touch of mischief in her tone. "Given that she was just upstairs with a guy, innocence doesn't exactly seem to be the word for it."

The interplay of mystics and innocence wove together in my thoughts, forming a complex tapestry of bewilderment. It felt as though each passing day unveiled new layers of this mystical realm's intricacies.

Eliza found herself immersed in a world of mystics and witches, all while I grappled with this newfound role as some kind of mystic combatant. Yet, the path ahead was rife with challenges, especially given the propensity for both Jared and Eliza's mother to withhold critical information. With a graceful leap, Jared perched himself on the arm of the couch, his gaze intent as he met Eliza's, his expression laden with seriousness.

"Innocence acts as a lure for corrupt mystics. The shifter we encountered was one of those corrupted ones. Mystics are divided into two categories: pure and corrupt. The pure ones reside in a realm known as Ellevil, separate from our own."

The notion of Ellevil was a fleeting thought; Eliza's focus was drawn to the dichotomy between pure and corrupt mystics. The idea that benevolent mystics existed somewhere brought a measure of comfort. But the question remained – why did the corrupt ones sow chaos in her world? It appeared that witches played a role in restoring order, eliminating these mystical threats.

"Could you expand on what you mean by innocence?" Eliza's inquiry was tinged with genuine interest.

Jared's sigh held a note of exasperation. "If you'd allow me to explain, I would. Innocence is akin to radiating happiness, carefree optimism, and an unwavering pursuit of excellence. It's a quality that draws the attention of corrupt mystics, who seek to tarnish and distort those virtues." He glanced momentarily at the bookcase, then refocused on Eliza and Dawn.

With a fluid motion, Jared leaped onto the couch, his posture conveying the weight of his words. "This is how witches perceive innocence. Anyone can possess it. Eliza, as a new witch, you might not fully embody that innocence just yet." Jared hopped down, used his nose to rummage through Eliza's purse, and retrieved her broomstick. Returning to them, he placed it on the couch's arm. "Newcomers like you are more susceptible to corruption compared to experienced witches."

His paw pressed the button on the broomstick, causing it to shrink. Jared's unwavering gaze remained fixed on Eliza, briefly disrupted by Dawn's interjection. Stepping forward, Dawn locked eyes with Jared as she spoke.

As for Eliza, a growing curiosity arose about how to rid herself of this unsettling trace that attracted mystics. She even considered resorting to multiple showers a day in hopes of finding a solution.

"Jared, I'm confident Eliza will be fine. She just took down a mystic!"

Jared's response carried a trace of skepticism. "With my guidance. She wasn't entirely ready to finish the task. She has a long way to go."

Eliza's determination to defend herself emerged. "I was scared, okay? I didn't know what to do. Give me a break. I'm not exactly like Mom."

Her dagger lay on the floor, and Eliza retrieved it, her gaze fixed on the shifter's blood staining its edge. She surveyed the room, taking in the aftermath of the mystic's intrusion.

As she returned the broomstick to her purse, a surreal realization dawned upon her – a mystic had infiltrated her sanctum. The thought lingered – how many times had she unknowingly brushed shoulders with mystics hidden behind human façades?

"That's exactly why you're not ready to handle a full-on party crowd, especially with mystics on the loose," Jared said, casting glances between Eliza and Dawn. He made his way over to his cat bed, giving it a nudge to reveal a strange syringe-like contraption, reminiscent of something out of a sci-fi movie. "I'll help get rid of that horrid memory, Dawn."

"Whoa, hold up! This is some Men in Black stuff. Please, no memory erasing here. I want to remember all this. If I ever find myself in danger again, I want to be there to back up Eliza," Dawn exclaimed, her tone a mix of both excitement and apprehension.

Despite the recent brush with danger, Dawn seemed oddly invigorated by the chaos, eager to embrace the adventure. Eliza couldn't help but feel conflicted; she wanted to shield Dawn from the perils of her supernatural life, but she also understood the appeal of having a trusted friend at her side.

"Too risky, Dawn. You're not a witch like her. You can't just take on mystics. Only she has that power," Jared hissed, his worry palpable.

Dawn's gaze softened as she bit her lip, her attention fixed on Jared. "But... please?"

"Jared, I think Dawn could be a great support for me when things get dicey again. Maybe she can knock some sense into me, like you did," Eliza interjected, her voice carrying a hint of earnestness.

While Eliza's protective instincts urged her to shield Dawn from danger, she also recognized the strength that came from having a friend who truly understood the twists and turns of her unconventional life.

"Do you really want to put your friend's life on the line once more? Remember, I won't always be there, Eliza. Nor will your mother," Jared's voice carried a note of concern, his frustration evident. He was well aware of the potential risks and the limits of his protection, and the fear of losing those he cared for weighed heavily on him. Dawn's presence had become an integral part of their lives, making her safety a priority.

"I promise, I won't let a mystic harm Dawn, ever! How can you even think that?" Eliza's voice quivered with a mix of determination and exasperation. The thought of Dawn being in danger was unbearable, and Eliza's fierce protectiveness shone through.

"I'm merely posing the 'what if,' Eliza. What if?" Jared's response carried a hint of sternness, his concern for their safety driving his words.

It was clear that Jared's nerves were frayed, and Eliza couldn't blame him. He had been entrusted with their safety, and the idea of them being exposed to danger weighed heavily on him. Dawn had essentially become a part of their makeshift family, adding an extra layer of responsibility.

"But I'm a witch, Jared, and I'm still learning. Once I've mastered my abilities, there won't be any room for mercy." Eliza's declaration carried a sense of conviction, her determination to protect Dawn unwavering.

Jared's eyes remained fixed on Eliza, his whiskers twitching as he observed their conversation. His gaze shifted between Eliza and Dawn, and then Eliza carefully retrieved the syringe, placing it back beneath Jared's bed.

Eliza's thoughts churned as she grappled with the recent confrontation. The battle with the wolf had rattled her more than witnessing her mother vanquish the fairy. Being a witch was an ongoing journey, and she was still learning to harness her instincts, to strike the balance between caution and courage.

"I trust my instincts, Jared," Eliza declared, her words a reflection of newfound resolve. The tension in the room seemed to ease, a sense of understanding settling in. Eliza's words seemed to offer reassurance, alleviating some of Jared's worries about her attending the rave alone. The desire to prove herself and her growing abilities was strong, and Eliza knew that this transformation process required her to navigate challenges independently.

"If you're feeling him, then go for it. If not, well, it's your call," Dawn's voice held an easygoing vibe as she adjusted her hair in the car's rearview mirror. "Just live a little, girl." A laugh danced in her tone, carrying the excitement of the unknown. "And hey, if Eric turns out to be some kind of mystical dude, don't hesitate to take care of business. You've got this!"

Eliza was caught in a whirlwind of emotions, her thoughts racing as they cruised down the road. The store "Bad Kitty" came into view, its bold black and pink signage beckoning them. A mix of curiosity and uncertainty swirled within her.

She couldn't shake the feeling that the store might be a bit too wild for her taste. Yet, Dawn's enthusiasm for all things witchy was contagious, and Eliza could see her best friend was ready to dive headfirst into whatever arcane escapade awaited.

Dawn's unwavering support and her zest for life were like a safety net around Eliza's heart. An urge to shield Dawn from danger tugged at her, amplified by the fact that Dawn seemed to attract mystics without even trying, thanks to her natural innocence. It was a double-edged sword, but it was also a unique strength that could be harnessed. Eliza felt a mix of responsibility and determination to navigate this mystical world with Dawn by her side.

As they approached each new twist on this journey, Eliza's determination to equip herself grew stronger. The lack of formal training was not going to hold her back.

Her trusty broomstick, versatile and reliable, was a symbol of her growing power, and her grimoire held a treasure trove of knowledge about mystics and their ways. The thought of facing these creatures was daunting, but it didn't deter Eliza's determination to learn, to evolve, and to stand her ground.

Eliza's determination radiated, echoing through her thoughts. She was entering a new phase in her life, carving out a path as a witch, much like she had navigated her way without her father's presence. If she could manage life without him, she believed she could certainly tackle this new mystical journey on her own.

Clutching the car door handle, Eliza's knuckles turned white with anticipation. Her gaze was fixed on the tinted windows of the store, her eyes narrowing to make out the details beyond. Her fingers found solace around her broomstick, tucked safely in her purse. She wished it had been by her side when she confronted the mystic at home.

Frustration bubbled within her. What good was a potent weapon if she couldn't wield its power? The sky overhead matched her mood, a storm brewing once again. She pulled her hoodie tight over her head, ready to face whatever lay ahead. Dawn's chatter about the store and her rave outfit had accompanied them throughout the ride, filling the air with a mix of excitement and nervous energy.

Skipping ahead to the edge of the sidewalk, Dawn's playful call broke through Eliza's thoughts. "Come on, slow poke!" she sang.

Eliza closed her car door and quickened her pace to catch up with Dawn, who was already at the store's entrance.

"Hey, Katie!" Dawn greeted the woman behind the register, clearly a familiar face. She had formed a bond with the store's employees, a testament to her infectious personality.

Taking in the store's interior, Eliza felt a sense of enchantment wash over her. Glittering strings hung from the ceiling like ethereal vines, guiding her deeper into the shop. Along the black carpet, a row of furry boots lined up, ready for attention. The store's aesthetic was a far cry from Eliza's initial assumptions. Dawn's influence had made her expect something wildly different, perhaps even a bit risqué. She shivered at the thought.

Moving past an array of colorful skirts, Eliza's fingers brushed lightly over their textures. Tops and skimpy bikinis were scattered around, an array of neon colors and fur captivating her gaze. Her bewilderment gave way to curiosity.

"Alright, let's start with your outfit," Eliza gestured towards Dawn and the surrounding selection.

Dawn's eyes sparkled with anticipation. "What's with all the fur and neon colors?" she quipped, a mixture of amusement and intrigue in her voice.

In a store ablaze with vibrant colors and funky attire, Dawn's enthusiasm was palpable. "Silly bean, you're in a rave store! Well, more like a go-go dancer store. It's where they go to get their outfits," she explained with animated gestures, her arms outstretched like her mom's whenever she delved into something she loved. A cascade of colorful outfits cascaded into Eliza's arms as Dawn tossed them her way, eager to see her friend try them on.

Inside the fitting room, Eliza's gaze fell upon her reflection, her body standing awkwardly before her. She contemplated her figure – not extremely slender, nor notably heavy. Unsure of where she fit on the spectrum, she grappled with her self-image.

A twinge of insecurity gnawed at her as she noticed a small patch of flesh spilling over her sides. A desperate desire to shed those imperfections gnawed at her, yet her body seemed resistant to change, unresponsive to her efforts to tone up.

Emerging from the fitting room, Eliza hesitated, modeling the chosen outfit for Dawn. As she looked to her friend for approval, Dawn's head shook in gentle disapproval, a signal to try something different. The discarded outfit hit the floor as Eliza slipped into a bikini. Gazing at herself in the mirror, the light blue bikini with delicate pink lines accentuating its contours caught her eye.

Dawn swung the door open, her jaw practically hitting the floor in astonishment. "This one is so perfect for you!" she squealed, waving her hands excitedly.

Uncertainty tugged at Eliza as she assessed her reflection. "I don't know... Wearing something like this won't exactly help me blend in," she murmured, her voice tinged with doubt.

The thought of drawing attention was daunting. Unwanted gazes and whispers had a way of making her retreat inward, shielding herself from prying eyes. Amid the allure of vibrant colors and lively patterns, the fear of standing out loomed large in her mind.

"It's fine," Dawn's voice chimed, though Eliza sensed that her words had fallen on distracted ears.

Dawn's attention was laser-focused on transforming her into a go-go dancer extraordinaire. "Seriously, you've got the body for it. Your hair, on the other hand..." Dawn playfully jabbed her fingers into Eliza's tangled locks, attempting to salvage some semblance of order as they both assessed the results in the mirror. "We'll work on that, no worries." Dawn let out a soft laugh. "Shoes!" she suddenly exclaimed, as if struck by inspiration. "I know just the pair." Without averting her gaze from Eliza, she yelled, "Katie!"

The shop assistant, Katie, promptly appeared in the fitting room doorway. "What can I do for you?" she inquired with a friendly smile.

Dawn launched into a spirited discourse about shoes, and Katie obliged by disappearing into the depths of the store. Dawn followed her with lively enthusiasm, trailing behind like a comet's tail. After a brief interlude, Dawn returned to the fitting room clutching a pair of large, furry boots – they resembled an upsized version of UGG boots.

Her grin was infectious. "These are something special. They were on hold for me, but they're absolutely meant for you."

Transaction complete, the duo exited the store. Dawn's energy was palpable as she skipped towards her car, and Eliza glanced at the bag in her hand before making her way over to the passenger door.

The clothes she had tried on were utterly outside her comfort zone. They lay far beyond the boundaries of her familiar bubble. It was a different look, an identity shift that felt foreign yet strangely exciting. As her reflection gazed back at her from the mirror, Eliza found herself embracing this divergence from her norm.

It wasn't her usual style. It wasn't her typical realm.

And yet, it was perfect.

CHAPTER EIGHT

Amid the tranquil embrace of the water, jagged rocks pressed against Eliza's damp back, a reminder of the world above. She watched as air bubbles gracefully danced upwards, breaking the surface tension with their fragile presence. Her vision blurred slightly as water surrounded her, cocooning her in its embrace. It was like a surreal dream, her surroundings shifting from solid ground to the fluid depths below.

Gentle ripples passed over her, a watery caress that contrasted with her growing unease. Blinking slowly, Eliza tried to make sense of her situation. She found herself submerged, an unexpected aquatic world unfolding around her. Panic crept in as her ankles remained bound, immobilized as if by an unseen force.

An attempt to move her arms yielded no results – they were ensnared in an unyielding grip. Seaweed, sinuous and trailing, wrapped itself around her legs with an almost possessive hold. Every movement was thwarted by the constricting tendrils, her struggles mirrored by the rippling sea plants.

An urgency to breathe set in, her chest tightening in a desperate plea for air. But the very element that should sustain her had become a stifling barrier. A strand of slimy seaweed clung to her lips, smothering her mouth and nose. It seemed as if the water itself had turned against her, a sinister transformation that threatened to consume her.

With each constriction, her body responded, her heartbeat slowing in response to the encroaching darkness. As the pressure mounted and the world blurred, she could feel herself letting go, surrendering to the depths that surrounded her. It was a resignation, an acknowledgment that she was overpowered and outmatched by the merciless forces of the water.

Closing her eyes, Eliza succumbed to the watery embrace, a sense of peace mingling with her fading consciousness. The ebb and flow of the underwater world carried her away, a silent submission to the unknown depths.

☆☆☆

Eliza's eyes snapped open, her breath coming in short bursts. It felt like she'd just escaped from being trapped underwater. She flung the covers off and glanced at her legs, relieved they weren't glued together. Her fingers touched her neck, her face, her hair, trying to confirm she was back in her room. She was drenched in sweat, the cold kind that sticks to your skin.

Jared hopped off his shelf and landed at the foot of her bed. He touched her knee with his paw, like he was trying to calm her down.

"Bad dream. You're okay," Jared said, his ear twitching a little.

"Yeah, just a dream," Eliza repeated, her voice shaky.

Jared gave her a reassuring look before hopping away.

It was Saturday, the day Dawn was picking her up to head to Virginia Beach. They planned to leave early, so they could have plenty of time to shop and eat. She reached for her phone to check the time. Then headed to her bathroom to freshen up and get ready for the day.

10:00 a.m.

Even on weekends, she couldn't sleep in. Waking up late always made her feel like she'd missed out on the whole day. She squinted at her phone, the screen too bright for her eyes right now.

"Whoa, must've really been out cold, huh?" Eliza's voice broke the silence, filled with disbelief.

"I wish," Jared's response came, his tone carrying a mix of dry humor and sarcasm.

"What?" Eliza's brows furrowed, her confusion evident.

Jared blinked, clearly taken aback by her sudden question. "Huh?" he mumbled, still trying to process.

Eliza rolled her eyes at his bewildered response. She bent down to retrieve the grimoire that her mother had given her for study, tucked beneath her bed. Settling onto her pillow, she crossed her legs and opened the tome. The pages, brittle and dry, fluttered open under her touch as she skimmed through the text, searching for the section dedicated to Mystics and their magical ilk.

After a moment, she located what she was looking for. The bold letters "Mystic" adorned the top of the page. As she began to read about various magical creatures, her gaze lingered on the section about faeries.

"In order to vanquish a fairy," she read aloud, "you must resist temptation and pierce both of its hearts. There's one located on the right and one on the left, right beneath the nipple. This act can only be accomplished with a broomstick or a dagger. Also, avoid inhaling a fairy's scent, for it can numb your emotions and lead you to your own demise."

"Man, that sounds like no easy feat," Eliza murmured, her mind replaying the nightmares she had about the corrupt fairy. Its alluring scent had been potent and hard to resist. The thought of avoiding such an enchanting fragrance seemed almost impossible.

The digital clock displayed 11:30 a.m., marking the passage of time as Eliza delved into the mystifying world of magic.

Eliza flipped the page and found herself immersed in the realm of mermaids. Instantly, images of Ariel from "The Little Mermaid" danced through her mind, evoking a soft chuckle. A grin tugged at her lips as she read the brief description beneath the title. Adjacent to a mermaid illustration, a scribbled note caught her attention.

"Mermaids are like, super gorgeous beings," she mused under her breath. Their unique trait – singing every word – was intriguing, drawing in unsuspecting prey with their enchanting melodies. Her eyes widened at the next line. "Wait, what? Most dangerous kind of mystic? Seriously?" The weight of that revelation pressed upon her heart as she read further.

11:45 a.m.

Her heart sank a bit at the gravity of the information. The notion that mermaids, with their captivating voices, could be the most perilous mystic kind was unsettling. The memory of Ariel's alluring voice, which had charmed her even as a kid, struck her. She mused about how something so beautiful could be used for such sinister purposes, just like the fairy tale she had known.

Gazing at her cell phone's display, she noted the time. It felt as if she had been engrossed in the book for an eternity. Every fascinating tidbit and helpful hint seemed to carry the wisdom of her great aunts and cousins, as if they were speaking directly to her, guiding her understanding of her identity and purpose. Yet, amid all this newfound knowledge, one burning question remained unanswered – the enigma of the mystical assassin role that had been thrust upon her.

Eliza's focus was deeply immersed in her newfound knowledge about mystics, a spellbinding world that stole away her sense of time. Swiftly, she slid the grimoire beneath her bed, her movements guided by a newfound sense of urgency. A flicker of self-awareness prompted her to dash into the bathroom, her attention turning to her reflection. Taking a critical look at her wild hair, she resolved to tame it for once.

Seizing a bottle of mousse, she dispensed the foamy liquid onto her hand and deftly worked it through her hair. As her hair gradually conformed, becoming wavy, she left the bathroom in pursuit of a different task. Reaching for the black Bad Kitty shopping bag, she extracted her furry outfit, her heart pounding with a blend of excitement and nerves. Taking a deep breath, she retreated into the bathroom.

The clock read 1:30 p.m.

A resounding honk pierced the air from outside, jolting Eliza from her preparations. Dawn, it seemed, was early by half an hour. Frantically, Eliza rummaged through her drawer, clothes flying until her hands landed on a tan cardigan embellished with jagged holes. Her bikini seemed to complement the cardigan perfectly, and a satisfied smile curved her lips.

"Perfect for the beach," she mused to herself.

Dawn's second honk echoed through the house, coaxing Eliza into action. Clutching her beach bag with care, she descended the stairs, her steps measured and cautious.

The clock struck 2:00 p.m.

A soft creak resonated through the house, otherwise veiled in silence. Eliza guessed that Jare, her feline companion, had ventured off somewhere. With a nonchalant shrug, she turned her attention to the door. Opening it, she was greeted by the sight of a sleek, black car with matching rims.

However, something felt off – this car was definitely not Dawn's.

Eliza's gaze fixated on the guy leaning casually against the vehicle, her eyes taking in every detail. His attire was laid-back, flip flops adorning his feet while his tanned skin shimmered under the sun's warm embrace.

Light blue shorts with stylish rips hugged his legs, and a certain ruggedness emanated from his clenched jaws and his strong, shirtless frame. Her breath escaped her lips in a soft exhale, the sight captivating her.

As he slowly moved towards Eliza, the gravel beneath his feet made a soft crunching sound, adding a subtle rhythm to his approach. A smirk graced his lips, and his rich chocolate eyes locked onto hers, sending a shiver down her spine.

An unspoken tension enveloped them, the air between their bodies growing taut. The scent of Hollister cologne drifted to her nose, and his touch beneath her chin made her heart race. Leaning in close, he whispered into her ear, his voice rough and enticing. "You're staring again, Miss Swift." His words sent a shiver through her, the sensation trailing down her skin like a cascade of goosebumps.

Eliza's thoughts raced, wondering how someone like Eric could be standing in front of her instead of Dawn. The realization of his presence left her bewildered – how did he know where she lived? Her lips parted hesitantly as she stammered, "I—I'm sorry."

His hand traced a slow path down her arm, a gentle touch that made her grip her beach bag tightly in her nervousness. As his fingers found hers, he loosened her grip with a subtle motion, his gaze still locked onto hers. Light green eyes stared back at her, their depth reflecting a hidden intensity.

Eric's response carried a hint of intrigue. "I didn't say I didn't like it." He smoothly took hold of her beach bag, interrupting her dazed thoughts. Her eyes lifted to his face, his closeness sending a flutter of nerves through her body. The contours of his muscular chest moved as he breathed, and veins traced the lines of his lean arms. She glanced down at her beach bag, a mix of emotions swirling within her.

"Hey, where's Dawn?" Eliza managed to utter, her gaze darting around the surroundings. A slight frown tugged at her lips as she reached for her phone, the intention to text her friend forming. But before she could do so, Eric intercepted, snatching the phone and slipping it into his pocket.

"Don't sweat it," Eric responded, a mischievous grin playing at the corners of his lips.

Eliza's eyes locked onto his face. "Give me my phone back, Eric."

He shrugged nonchalantly, taking a step back. "You want it? Come and get it."

With a cleared throat, Eliza turned on her heel and marched back up the steps to her house. Eric, however, wasn't about to let her go that easily. He looped an arm around her waist and turned her back around. An amused chuckle escaped him as he guided her towards his car, a gesture that was almost gentlemanly.

The new car smell surrounded her as she slid into the polished black leather seat. Eric closed the door gently, the smirk on his face ever-present. Her eyes closed, and she inhaled deeply. Swiftly, she reached into his pocket, swiping her phone.

"T think...this is my phone, thank you very much," Eliza declared, a touch of sass in her voice.

Glancing at the neighboring houses, her nerves seemed to ebb away in his presence. The once-intimidating atmosphere now felt strangely comfortable. It didn't matter how cute he might look – she held onto the realization that none of this was real.

As he pressed the car's start button, the rumble of the engine drew her attention back to him. His smile radiated warmth, and as he drove away, the sight of her house receding into the distance felt surreal.

She turned back in her seat, wrapping her cardigan around herself. It was then that the truth struck her anew – the one driving was Eric, and he seemed content to have her along for the night, a fact evident in the happiness that glowed in his eyes.

Eliza's voice carried a blend of surprise and accusation. "So, all of this was preplanned? You thought I wouldn't find out about this secret scheme of yours?" Her eyes were fixed on Eric, her tone a mixture of disbelief and mild irritation.

Eric met her gaze with a playful grin. "You're pretending like you had it all figured out. Come on, everyone deserves a surprise now and then. And, well, I had a feeling you missed me a bit too." His lips formed a teasing smirk.

A snort escaped Eliza's lips. "Sure thing," she replied with a roll of her eyes, a hint of sarcasm lacing her words. She shifted her attention to me, who was engrossed in my phone, scrolling through her apps.

"Feeling hungry?" Eric inquired, attempting to change the subject.

Eliza glanced at him before her gaze wandered to the crystal blue lights that danced across his skin, cast by the car's speedometer. The car's interior was dimly lit due to the tinted windows.

"Not really," she replied with a nonchalant shrug.

As if in response to her words, my stomach let out a rumbling growl that echoed through the car, betraying my true hunger. Heat rushed to my cheeks, embarrassed by the sudden noise. She quickly clamped her hands over her stomach and instinctively covered her mouth, avoiding making eye contact with Eric.

Eric couldn't help but chuckle. "Quite the fibber, huh? Hungry, then?"

Eliza's lips curved into a sheepish grin. "Well, maybe just a bit."

Eric's eyes sparkled with amusement. "Where should we grab a bite?"

A moment of hesitation passed before Eliza replied, "Sweet Frog, I guess."

His laughter mingled with her response. "You're a frozen yogurt fan?"

Eliza's smile widened. "Absolutely love it."

Eric's grin mirrored her enthusiasm. It was evident that he was delighted to share this dining choice with her. "Well, now we can enjoy some frozen yogurt before the rave."

A flicker of worry crossed Eliza's mind. "Won't we be late?"

Eric's grin turned confident. "Nah, my car's pretty speedy."

Eliza and Eric's destination was Central Plaza. It felt a bit like a smaller version of a market square, with an assortment of restaurants and compact shops filling the scene. They eventually snagged a parking spot, and Eric swiftly hopped out of the car to hold the door for Eliza.

This wasn't a date—no way, right? But then again, maybe it kind of was? Eliza's heart thudded in her chest as her mind raced to catch up. She repeated the mantra: don't panic. Her chest rose and fell in rhythm with her heartbeat. She could handle this. She totally could.

"Thanks," Eliza murmured, her lashes fluttering up as her lips curled into a shy grin. She tugged her long cardigan a bit more around herself, feeling a rush of warmth and nerves all at once. As they approached the store, his arm found its way around her, and she couldn't help but tense up at the contact of his half-bare skin against hers. Suppressing a grin, she shifted her attention forward, his gesture giving her a subtle boost.

Inside the store, it was hard to miss the eyes of the other customers who couldn't help but glance Eric's way. It might've been awkward, but at the moment, Eliza couldn't find it in her to care too much.

Tugging her cardigan more securely around her, she draped it over her rave outfit, determined not to draw even more attention to them. She had pulled on a pair of shorts to cover the lower part of her outfit. Gazing down, she noticed the blue and pink hues of the bikini peeking out from below. She noted that her shorts were unbuttoned, the zipper casually left open.

Making their way to the yogurt section, Eliza selected a cup of cookies and cream flavor. Eric opted for strawberry. It was a simple choice, but in that moment, amidst the quiet bustle of the store, it felt like another small step on their unexpected journey.

Eric dipped his index finger into his yogurt, his mischievous gaze set on Eliza. Swiftly, he aimed for her nose, but with a yelp, she dodged his attempt, a playful laughter escaping her lips. Determined, Eric managed to catch her, his arms encircling her waist from behind. His yogurt-coated finger found its target, and he licked off the creamy sweetness.

Grinning, he spoke softly, his words carrying a mix of playfulness and sincerity. "You can't escape me, you know. I'll always catch you."

With their frozen yogurts decked out in a colorful array of toppings, Eric took care of the bill. Eliza adorned hers with a shower of jelly beans, while he playfully scattered chocolate chips over hers. Finding a cozy spot by the window, they settled into their seats, perfect for two.

As Eliza's phone vibrated in her purse, a notification from Dawn illuminated her face. With a head shake and a smile at the text, Eliza stowed her phone away. Observing her reaction, Eric seized an opportunity and dipped his spoon into her yogurt.

"Got yogurt on my face?" Eric inquired, his hand reaching to his chin.

She chuckled. "No, just a text from Dawn." Eliza playfully denied it with a head shake.

"Dawn's been my guide," Eric admitted. "I wouldn't even have known where you live without her help, she gave me directions."

Eliza swirled her spoon in her yogurt, creating a pink mess that made her grin. She contemplated the mess, her thoughts taking a lighter turn.

"I'm going to get her for this," she muttered, her tone feigned annoyance.

Eric couldn't help but chuckle. "Hush now. And come on, let's be real, you're always on the move whenever we meet," he said, pausing to take a bite of his yogurt. "So, this was the perfect way to corner you into spending yogurt time with me." He looked up, his gaze meeting hers, a warm smile curving his lips.

Eliza met his gaze, her own smile matching his. "I'm not always running, you know."

He grinned back. "If you say so."

They chatted and chatted some more about Eric's life: the close call with his dog nearly sending him splashing into a lake, his preference for Slytherin in Harry Potter, and his unexpected love for math. Eliza wrinkled her nose playfully at that last bit. Amidst laughter, she couldn't help but notice the way his tiny freckles seemed to dance across the bridge of his nose.

"Slytherin, huh? I knew you were trouble."

"From the moment I walked in?" Eric responded with a teasing smirk.

"You're such a jerk." Eliza retorted, her laughter blending with the playful banter.

As they continued talking, time slipped away like sand through their fingers. Tears of joy welled up in Eliza's eyes from all the shared laughter. Unsure if it was an official date or not, their conversation flowed naturally, each moment feeling surprisingly effortless. For the first time in a while, she found herself genuinely enjoying the company.

Eventually, they left the store, yogurts unfinished, and stepped outside, heading towards Eric's car. Eliza's gaze lingered on his back, noticing the subtle flexing of his muscles. A grin tugged at her lips, a silent appreciation for the simple things.

A casual gesture brought Eliza's hand up to brush her hair away from her face, tucking it neatly behind her ear. She pursed her lips, deep in thought.

Perhaps, she mused, the male species wasn't all that bad after all.

10

―・―

CHAPTER NINE

Eric leaned casually against the car, propping the door open with one hand. Eliza's heart danced with a mixture of excitement and nerves, her thoughts running wild about whether he'd let her in with her stash of snacks. Drawing closer to his sleek ride, her fingers tightened around the cup of yogurt, but before she could even speak, Eric swooped in, swiping the cup from her hand and giving her a pointed look.

"No food allowed, sorry," he drawled, a smirk tugging at his lips.

"Seriously?" Eliza's eyebrows shot up.

"No," he chuckled, a mischievous glint in his eyes. With a quick, almost playful motion, he snatched the spoon from her grip and dipped it into the yogurt, taking a satisfying scoop. His words came out in a half-muffled, half-amused tone as he savored the treat.

A grin tugged at Eliza's lips, and she nudged him in the stomach with her elbow. He let out a mock grunt, and she seized the opportunity to slip into her seat, her laughter blending with the wind rustling through her hair.

"You always have to make an entrance, don't you?" she teased as she settled in.

"Was that necessary?" he shot back, the engine purring to life under his command.

"Yes. I attack thieves," she quipped, a glint of playfulness in her eyes.

"I was going to give it back," he countered with a laugh, his gaze meeting hers for a brief, electric moment.

"Sure," Eliza replied, her voice laced with playful skepticism.

Then, with a twist of the key and a confident rev of the engine, they were off. The car seamlessly merged onto the highway, the rush of wind hitting them as Eric deftly maneuvered into the fast lane. He rolled down the windows, allowing the cool breeze to sweep through the car, ruffling Eliza's hair. The radio's volume soared, and with a quick, practiced motion, he slipped on his shades, the world outside becoming a blur of speed and adventure.

As Eric's finger pressed down on the button, a magical transformation began. The roof of the car slowly lifted, and Eliza's eyes widened in surprise. The convertible before them was a thing of beauty, something she had only dreamed of. She gazed up at the sky, a canvas splashed with the hues of a fiery sunset – deep oranges, passionate reds, and soft pinks.

The sun dipped below the horizon with a graceful bow, casting a spell over the world.

Eliza couldn't contain her excitement. She threw her arms up in the air, letting out a scream that mingled perfectly with the wind's rush, muffling Eric's laughter. The wind was a powerful symphony, drowning out Eric's voice.

An exhilarating wave surged through both of them, their hearts pounding in sync. In that moment, they felt utterly free, as if the wind itself was carrying them to new heights. Their hair danced wildly in the wind, a testament to their exhilaration.

With one hand on the steering wheel, Eric guided the car effortlessly, a master of this newfound freedom. His other arm found solace outside the window, fingers trailing through the wind.

"This is absolutely incredible!" Eliza's voice carried on the wind.

"What?" Eric shouted back, struggling to hear.

"I said, this is incredible!" Eliza's words echoed in the wind.

Eric attempted a response, his words a soft murmur, but the wind stole them away, leaving only the rush of the moment.

☆☆☆

Time had a funny way of slipping away when you were caught up in the whirlwind of fun. The idea of being the first ones at the party didn't really register on their radar.

After all, it was a full-on rave they were heading to, and Eliza was pretty confident these things didn't kick off until well into the night. The world outside transformed from a dull backdrop into a vibrant kaleidoscope as they drove through it.

Off to the side, a Ferris wheel burst to life, adorned with swirling rainbow lights that seemed to bounce off everything around them. Eliza couldn't help but breathe in sharply, caught up in the sheer exuberance of it all. The bass from the music pulsed against their chests, and a carnival, all flashing lights and laughter, whizzed by in a blur.

On the boardwalk, people were streaming toward the colorful lights like moths drawn to a flame. Eric hit the gas, causing the car to lurch forward with a burst of speed. To the world zipping by on the bridge, they were no more than a fleeting shadow.

Eliza caught their own reflection on the surface of the ocean, the water reflecting back the glittering lights. The waves crashed against each other, casting sparkling ripples that sent a thrill down their spine. It was a heady mix of excitement and nerves, aching to break free from the confines of the car.

With a gradual ease, Eric slowed the car down and steered it into a sandy parking lot. The wind, the rush, the whole wild scene had Eliza's body practically buzzing.

Eliza had never known happiness like this before. In this moment, it was as if every worry had faded, replaced by an overwhelming sense of joy that bubbled up from deep within.

Eliza's date skillfully found a parking spot, and then Eric courteously opened her door, extending his hand. With a simple touch of a button, the trunk of the car sprang open. Eliza playfully skipped over to it and rummaged through her beach bag. Spotting her broomstick, memories of Jared's words echoed in her mind.

"Stay out of the crowd," Eliza recalled Jared's advice.

She shrugged, sighed, and retrieved the special white boots that Dawn had given her. The sand had already started infiltrating her flip flops, and she knew it would upset Dawn if she caught Eliza not wearing the boots. Sliding her feet into them, she wrapped her cardigan around her waist to complete the look.

As Eliza shut the trunk, she turned around and caught Eric staring at her, his expression a mixture of astonishment and disbelief. His mouth hung open in shock, and he looked like he might start drooling any moment.

"Wow, you're glowing!" Eric exclaimed, his finger pointing in her direction.

Eliza glanced down at her outfit, noticing that the baby pink outlines on the fabric were indeed radiating under the moonlight. Unable to contain her delight, she twirled around, a smile lighting up her face. She had no idea that her attire was made from glow-in-the-dark material.

With a confident stride, Eliza approached Eric, whose mouth still remained agape. Playfully, she slid her index finger under his chin, lightly tickling his facial hair, and then gently closed his mouth.

"You're staring," Eliza teased, a smirk tugging at her lips.

Eric burst into laughter and unexpectedly scooped Eliza off the ground.

"Hey, put me down!" Eliza protested, her voice carrying a mixture of laughter and surprise.

"No way," Eric responded, his grin infectious.

Approaching the massive crowd, the energy in the air was electric, almost palpable. Eric set Eliza down gently, and they stood side by side, their eyes wide with wonder as they took in the scene before them.

Among the dancing throng, guys shirtless and splattered with paint moved in sync with girls sporting colorful bras, creating a kaleidoscope of movement and color. The urge to join in the lively spectacle bubbled within them. Eric's biting his lip revealed his excitement, and he held out his hand for Eliza to take.

Amidst the chaotic beauty, paint burst into the air, a cascade of color that sent ripples of cheers through the crowd. The participants danced and reveled, utterly carefree. Three adventurous souls sprinted towards the ocean, jumping into the waves with abandon. Eliza couldn't help but feel a pang of concern for their safety amidst the wild revelry.

Eric's grip on her hand was strong, his enthusiasm contagious as he led her into the heart of the dancing crowd. They leapt and bounced, their voices mingling with the pulsating music. The DJ had spun Icona Pop into a dubstep remix, adding an extra layer of energy to the atmosphere. Eric settled behind Eliza, his solid presence giving her a comforting support as her head rested against his jawline.

Amidst the joyful chaos, laughter and shrieks filled the air as girls brushed past Eliza. The rhythm flowed through them, an irresistible current pulling them along. The bass pounded, each beat a synchronized thud in tune with Eliza's racing heart. The vibrations coursed through her skin, leaving a tingling trail in their wake.

In an unexpected twist, two girls burst onto the scene, drawing everyone's attention. One playfully pecked the DJ's cheek, earning a grin from him.

The other dancer became the heart of the stage, her graceful movements captivating the crowd. Her hips swayed in time with the music, and her long hair spun like a mesmerizing vortex. With infectious enthusiasm, she guided the audience, beckoning them to follow her lead.

Unable to resist the contagious energy, Eric and Eliza jumped along with the dancer, their feet sending sand into the air as they matched the growing intensity of the music. The beat slowed momentarily, building suspense before unleashing a tidal wave of bass and exhilarating dubstep vibrations that seemed to resonate in their very bones.

The song suddenly stopped, and the crowd quieted down. Then, out of nowhere, a huge wave of bass and vibrations hit them, making Eliza burst out laughing.

Onstage, the dancer's routine changed. She glided across the floor, did a cool move with her neck, and twirled around. She even stuck her tongue out and smiled. Then she went to the other side of the stage, giving a high-five to her friend who had kissed the DJ.

The dancer kept moving her hips to the beat, and then Eliza realized that it was Dawn. Seeing Dawn dance like that looked so effortless. Suddenly, Eliza felt something wet on her back. It was paint. More splashes followed, and Eliza just laughed, jumping around and letting her hair fly.

Three girls came around Eliza, dancing and twirling along with the music. They were kind of grinding against her. They smelled like the ocean. The girl in front of Eliza had a neon outfit on and a big smile. Her wavy hair went down to her belly and had these cool color changes from red to pink.

Eliza looked down the girl's hair and saw the colors shifting. The girl on her left had a similar thing going on with her hair. Dark green at the top that turned into a lighter green. The girl twirling behind Eliza had dark blue hair that faded into light blue. They all moved to the music, and then they went away, disappearing into the crowd and heading towards the ocean.

Eliza brushed her hair out of her face, feeling this strong urge inside. She wanted to follow those girls, to be carefree like them. In that moment, she wished she could dance just like they did, throwing herself into the music and the energy of everything around her.

Eliza spotted three girls skipping along the shore, moving in perfect sync. They twirled, giggled, and threw sand in the air, like a glittering storm. Their bikinis, stretched tight, glowed like they were from another world, all while they danced in the sand cloud.

In the midst of it all, a faraway song caught Eliza's attention. The noise from the party seemed to fade, leaving only the beautiful voice calling her. It was like everything else vanished, and only that voice mattered.

The three girls stopped their sandy play and looked up at Eliza, their lips moving slowly as they sang. Even from a distance, their words reached her ears. Eliza's glasses, usually not see-through, turned clear, revealing a new view.

"Pretty girls like you are a must," the girl with red hair said, putting her finger to her lips. "Come be luscious, like us. We're three you can trust," the green-haired girl giggled. "Along the shore. Come forth." The trio twirled gracefully. "Don't be shy. Come play with us," the blue-haired girl added, tossing sand with her hands as they sang.

Eliza felt pulled in, wanting to join their dance, to be part of what they were feeling. She felt a mix of excitement and longing.

As time went on, Eliza's smile became permanent, her cheeks starting to hurt from grinning so much. She desperately wanted to get their attention, to call out to them as they jumped into the water. But no matter how hard she tried, no sound came out. Her voice was worn out from cheering for the DJ earlier.

Eliza's heart raced, torn between the enchanting mermaids' dance and the frustration of not being able to make a sound.

Eliza raced after them, coming to a halt right at the water's edge. The big white boots were kicked off and cast aside, landing with a thud on the sand. The mist from the water sprayed against Eliza's glow-in-the-dark outfit, and the gentle waves tickled the tips of her toes. The girls' singing grew louder, an irresistible pull that Eliza couldn't ignore.

Eliza attempted to piece together a memory related to this scene, but the allure of the singing and dancing seemed to cloud those recollections. Frustration crept in, and Eliza's hands shot up to cover her ears, as if attempting to grasp at elusive memories.

Even as Eliza fought against the urge, the ocean's call was too strong. The water beckoned, a dark and inviting expanse. The sparkling waves swirled around her ankles, rising to her knees. Before long, they splashed against her thighs, a gentle but insistent push.

"Come play with us..." the girls' voices rang out.

They giggled, their words like a playful command. "Closer, keep walking."

A sudden splash kissed Eliza's face, the taste of salt lingering on her lips. In the midst of the splash, something grasped at Eliza's arm, an unseen force pulling her with swift determination. Before she could react, she was yanked through the cold water, her speed akin to lightning, until she found herself surrounded by the depths of the ocean.

Releasing Eliza's arm, the girl with fiery red hair turned in the water, facing Eliza with a graceful bounce. Moonlight painted her skin and hair with an ethereal glow, a soft shimmer that highlighted her beauty. Her smile was playful, and she bit her lip before letting her arms sway in rhythm with the gentle waves.

Eliza couldn't help but be enchanted by her appearance. She was breathtaking.

With a fluid motion, the red-haired girl began to spin in place, her eyes locking onto Eliza's as she circled back. Eliza's shock rooted her in place, her voice rendered useless from the hours of raving.

On each side of the girl's arms, delicate fins caught the moonlight, shining against the water's surface. Small gills on her cheeks moved with her breath, a mesmerizing and otherworldly sight.

Fear began to tighten its grip on Eliza's heart as the realization sank in. She wanted to scream, to let out her fear, but her voice failed her. In a swift, blurred movement, the girl twirled in the water, the sharp fin brushing against Eliza's neck.

The truth hit Eliza like a tidal wave, flooding her with disbelief and terror. She felt the scream welling up within her, but before it could escape, the girl's hand clamped onto Eliza's neck, silencing her.

Eliza's heart raced, her pulse a wild rhythm as she stared into the girl's pitch-black eyes. Between clenched teeth, the mermaid sang a haunting melody, its eerie notes laced with a command that sent shivers down Eliza's spine. A single drop of blood, slick and red, fell onto the water's surface – Eliza's blood – a stark, chilling reminder of the peril she was in.

Eliza's gaze lifted slowly, locking onto the girl's eyes. In a swift motion, the girl made a small cut on Eliza's throat, enough to send a jolt of discomfort through her but not causing any pain. To Eliza's surprise, the sensation was strangely absent.

Below them, a shadowy figure emerged from beneath, drawing closer. With a melodic hum, the girl's lips curved into a smile as she continued her eerie tune. Eliza's breath hitched as a sharp, triangular fin broke the water's surface, conjuring images of a massive shark closing in.

Catching Eliza's fear, the mermaid's smile only widened, her index finger playfully touching her lips before she brushed against Eliza's feet with an oddly intimate gesture.

Eliza felt a numbness spread through her, struggling to process the bizarre reality around her. Driven by a surge of instinct, Eliza's thoughts scrambled for a plan, her logical mind giving way to raw urgency.

In a heartbeat, Eliza lunged, jabbing her elbow at the mermaid's face. A melodic cry escaped the mermaid's lips as she splashed away, her form blending with the ripples of the water. Eliza swiftly turned, spotting the shore not too far away. Concerns about attracting sharks faded into insignificance as Eliza's singular focus shifted to escape, to finding solid ground.

Eliza swam with fervor, each stroke carrying her closer to safety. Her mind was a chorus of determination, the idea of reaching the shore a beacon of hope. Arms slicing through the water, legs kicking with force against the waves, Eliza battled the currents. A backward glance revealed the shark's fin, a stark reminder of the peril she was fleeing from.

Almost there. Just a bit more. Eliza kept swimming.

Eliza's breathing came in rapid, shallow bursts, her heart racing so fast it felt like it might burst from her chest. Air was a desperate need, an ache that consumed her every thought. The mermaids were after her, and panic coursed through her veins, driving her forward.

The cut on her throat stung with a fiery intensity, and her feet were like anchors, dragging her down. The shore was her lifeline; she had to reach it, no matter what.

"Don't think, just go," Eliza urged herself, her mind racing as fast as her body.

The vibrant lights of the rave glowed ahead, a distant promise of safety and solace. Eliza could feel the sand beneath her feet, a reassuring touch even as she remained soaked from the water.

With every ounce of strength, Eliza propelled herself through the water, each stroke a battle against the resistance. As the shore neared, she felt a mixture of exhaustion and determination, a sense of relief washing over her as her feet finally found solid ground.

Eliza thought she was safe.

But then, just as she tried to let out a cry for help, the water muffled her voice, swallowing her words like they were nothing. "H-Help!" Eliza's plea was lost in the splashes and churn of the waves, her arms flailing as she coughed and struggled, the vast expanse of the sea muffling her desperate call for assistance.

"Please," Eliza's voice choked out, the word a desperate plea. Water seeped into her mouth as she fought for breath. "Help—" Her words were swallowed by the crashing waves, and before she could react, something strong gripped her ankles, dragging her forcefully underwater. "Come back... and play," the collective snarl of the mermaids sent a shiver down her spine.

Eliza's scream was silenced by the water that engulfed her, her hands flailing as she fought against the pull. Another tight grasp latched onto her ankle, intensifying the force dragging her down. The sea seemed determined to claim her.

A surge of panic surged through her veins, her body responding to the terror that gripped her. Her instinct was to fight, to free herself from the mermaids' grip, but the pressure in her chest made it hard to focus. Desperation urged her to use her hands to shield her mouth from the water, even as her body writhed in the depths.

Struggling against the mermaids' hold, Eliza's efforts were futile as their grip remained firm, their fingers digging into her skin. Suppressing the urge to scream, she recognized that a sound would lead to her drowning.

The world around her grew darker as the ocean's pressure distorted her senses, leaving her feeling disoriented. Amidst the turmoil, she was dragged through a forest of seaweed, the rough rocks and sharp leaves adding to her discomfort.

Suddenly, her movement ceased, and Eliza found herself suspended within the embrace of the seaweed. Fear held her paralyzed, a sense of helplessness washing over her.

A strand of red hair brushed against her cheek, a chilling reminder of the mermaids' presence. Another burst of color flashed before her eyes, followed by yet another as they circled her, an eerie dance that felt like a prelude to something far more sinister.

The water's gentle dance halted, holding its breath as the girl with fiery red hair glided through the liquid realm, a graceful vision suspended before Eliza's wide eyes.

There was something enchantingly unearthly about her – no telltale tail trailed behind, but her hair cast a shimmering glow, and her skin caught and scattered the light, conjuring an effervescent spectacle. Her fingers, adorned with long nails, brushed the water's surface, while her eyes, a deep, entrancing black, remained fixed on Eliza.

A soft, lilting whisper slipped into Eliza's thoughts, like a melody carried on the breeze, originating from the girl with sapphire-blue hair. "Why not take part in our game? Escape may prove futile, but the chase itself holds a joy all its own," the voice encouraged, its musical rhythm playing with Eliza's senses. Struggling against her liquid confines, Eliza's limbs remained stubbornly still, trapped as if by an unseen web.

Laughter, light as the wind's caress, trickled into Eliza's mind from the girl with emerald-green hair. "How intriguing! Has fear truly found its way to a witch's heart? I had imagined them braver," she chimed, twirling with carefree grace amidst the watery embrace.

A symphony of laughter surged, then silenced abruptly. The girl with blazing red locks cast a piercing stare Eliza's way, her fingers dancing through her damp hair before launching herself towards Eliza with an otherworldly swiftness.

Her movement flowed like a haunting melody, a testament to her affinity for the aquatic world. Arms outstretched, a fierce determination twisted her features as she surged through the embrace of the water.

Then, in an unexpected turn, a shadowy figure materialized, hurtling towards the red-haired mermaid. A motion, and glinting silvery darts were set free, carving shimmering arcs through the water. Lithe and nimble, the mermaid's form twisted with the grace of a dancer, her evasive maneuvers brushed with an almost uncanny instinct.

Within the watery arena, she performed a fluid somersault, her body's grace reminiscent of a spinning top. As the figure's silvery assault subsided, she dipped beneath its presence, and with a resonant snarl that rippled through the water, she struck back, her nails leaving behind a retaliatory trace against her adversary.

Pain radiated through Eliza's legs as relentless nails sank in, dragging her downward into the abyss.

Against a backdrop of jagged rocks, Eliza lay sprawled, her breath creating a trail of escaping air bubbles that danced towards the water's surface. The world around her became a watery haven, enveloping her completely. But her feet were unresponsive, numb from the chill. Frustrated attempts to move her arms yielded no results – they were locked in a stubborn grip.

Serpentine seaweed slithered around her legs, coiling with a vice-like grip, fusing them into a single entity. The impulse to breathe became desperate, yet her mouth was sealed by a single, clinging strand of seaweed.

The plant's tenacious hold constricted her, momentarily pausing her heart. Futility forced her to cease the struggle. With her eyes shut tight, she fought back the rising tide of panic, clutching at the edges of her resolve. A distant muffled scream reached her ears, jolting her from within.

Wide-eyed, she witnessed the figure thrust a weapon into the grasp of the girl with emerald-green hair, who clung to her legs. The green-haired girl, defiance etched across her features, retaliated by conjuring a tempestuous water tornado. Nature's fury clashed with an eerie calmness, an aquatic ballet of vengeance.

Eliza's attempts at resistance faltered, the odds stacked against her.

Amidst the turmoil, the figure lunged once more, their weapon finding purchase in the girl's stomach. She dissolved, fragmenting into an ethereal cascade of light-green bubbles that ascended towards the surface. Swift, decisive fingers found a red button, summoning forth a broomstick from thin air.

And in that moment, reality seemed to bend and twist, leaving Eliza grasping at the fringes of understanding.

The girl with red hair let out a piercing screech, her strokes through the water quickening with newfound urgency. Simultaneously, the figure in the water came to an abrupt halt, seemingly stunned by the ear-splitting noise. It crumpled and floated on the water's surface, unmoving.

With a triumphant smile, the mermaid glided forward, her graceful form effortlessly navigating the water as she closed in on Eliza. In one swift motion, she seized hold of Eliza's head and hurled it against a jagged rock positioned behind her.

The world faded to black.

11

CHAPTER TEN

"Eliza!" A hoarse voice called out, tinged with frustration. "Darn it!"

"Oh my God, is she alright?"

Eliza's body had somehow made its way to the surface, carried by the waves and deposited onto the sandy shore. Wet sand clung stubbornly to her cheeks and lips, a gritty reminder of her ordeal. Fingers clenched and dug into the ground, seeking an anchor.

A thumb brushed gently over her face, sweeping away the crusty residue and freeing her vision. Eric, his disbelief apparent, rushed to offer solace. He helped her sit up on the chilly sand.

Above her, Eric panted, his warm breath tickling the tip of her nose. Water-soaked and with flecks of wet sand sticking to his abs, his chest rose and fell rhythmically.

As the reality of why Eliza had ended up in the water sank in, she wriggled and twisted on the sand, her movements frantic, mingled with cries of distress. Overwhelmed by the shock of surviving, she spasmed in a mix of awe and disbelief.

"Help! I can't breathe," Eliza's voice cracked with urgency, her hands flying to her throat instinctively.

"Eliza, you're safe," Eric reassured, his arms enveloping her in a comforting embrace.

"The water... how did I get into the water," she muttered, her mind struggling to piece together the puzzle of her memories.

With careful hands, Eric picked off the remnants of seaweed that clung to Eliza's body, brushing away the ocean's remnants. Her neon baby pink outfit still glowed with an eerie light, a vestige of the night's earlier events. Her gaze shifted, catching sight of Dawn, who knelt nearby in her rave attire, a fellow survivor of the tumultuous night.

"I was chilling on stage, and I realized you and Eric had disappeared," Dawn explained, her tone comforting as she tried to ease Eliza's worries. "I remembered seeing you in your outfit, with Eric nearby."

"I went to find her," Eric interjected sharply, his gaze meeting Dawn's.

Was Eric the figure in the water?

"You dashed towards the shore. I spun around and you were gone in a flash. I tried to catch up, but the crowd was just chaos," Eric recounted, his frustration evident.

So, he wasn't the one in the water.

Eliza instinctively touched her throat, half-expecting the cut to still sting. But there was nothing there. Her gaze drifted to her legs, searching for any traces of the nail marks that had held her captive.

There was nothing to be found.

With cautious fingers, Eliza checked the back of her head, expecting to feel some lingering pain.

There were no signs of the watery ordeal on her skin. Her eyes locked onto Eric's, but he looked away, an uncomfortable tension in the air. A thin line of crimson painted his neck, contrasting against his complexion. He avoided her gaze, his discomfort palpable.

"You're injured," Eliza murmured, her focus fixed on him. Scratches adorned the side of his belly.

Eric caught her stare and quickly shifted his position. "It's just paint," he shrugged casually, turning his attention towards Dawn.

"Oh, I get it now," Eliza muttered, a lightbulb of understanding flickering on.

With the support of Eric and Dawn, Eliza got back on her feet, the cold, damp sand giving way beneath her. Eric guided her back to his car and swung open the door. "Are you absolutely sure you don't want me to come with?" Dawn asked, concern etched in his expression.

"It's okay, Dawn," Eliza managed a small smile.

"Go and enjoy yourself," Eric reassured her.

Dawn hesitated. "Are you sure? I could totally talk to my manager, get off early. Seriously, I--."

"I'm good, Dawn. I'm just glad you're happy with your job," Eliza replied.

Dawn nibbled on her lip, casting a meaningful glance at Eliza. "Cellphone?"

"Handled," Eric's reply had a hint of dry humor.

"I'm speaking to Eliza. You'll call me, right?" Dawn threw a final look Eliza's way before stepping backwards.

"For sure!" Eliza nodded.

"Take care of her, or I might consider drowning you next," Dawn stated seriously, her gaze shifting from Eliza to Eric, a stern expression settling on her face. Eric squared his shoulders, assisting Eliza into the car, while Dawn retraced her steps toward the lively crowd of ravers.

Eric settled behind the wheel, starting the car's engine. He hit the start button, activating the sunroof. The soft blue lights traced patterns on his skin once more.

Eliza shut her eyes for a moment, and when she opened them, they were gliding through her neighborhood, the car coming to a stop in front of her house.

They both got out and made their way up the steps to Eliza's home. "So, what did you think of the rave?" Eric asked, breaking the silence.

"It was... interesting, and fun. I was having a great time until things got crazy," Eliza said as she fished out her keys from her purse, while Eric waited patiently.

"I hope you won't let this spoil our plans down the line," Eric's voice held a mix of sincerity and something more, a note of hidden meaning that caught Eliza's attention. She looked at him, her eyes searching his, as she unlocked the door.

Eric narrowed his eyes, his gaze locked onto Eliza. "You're not gonna let me see where you live?" he asked, his tone curious, tinged with a touch of expectation. Eliza hesitated, her mind racing to the mess she'd made with the mystic earlier. Holding onto the doorknob, she took a deep breath, then turned around – only to accidentally bump into Eric's chest.

In an instant, his hands reached out to steady her at her sides. "Sorry," Eliza mumbled, feeling flustered. "It's just that... well..."

"Don't worry about the mess. Most places are messy. I just want to check out your place," Eric reassured her, a small smile tugging at the corner of his lips.

Eliza's mind raced, brainstorming excuses for the scratches on the wall. She was relieved that there was no trace of blood or gore on the carpet, but those scratches still made her anxious.

"It's really not a big deal," Eric said, his fingers tilting her chin gently, as if he was about to kiss her. Eliza's heart raced, and she instinctively stepped back, putting some space between them. Eric chuckled softly, and she quickly turned to open her door.

In her peripheral vision, Eliza spotted Jare waiting in the hallway. She could only imagine he'd heard the conversation. Taking a quick look at the wall, she sighed with relief – the scratches were gone.

The furniture was in place, and the place looked as clean as ever. However, Jared's body language wasn't as cheerful. His tail was down as he eyed the man behind her. With a jingle of his necklace, he scampered upstairs.

But then, out of nowhere, a sharp crackle of electricity sliced through the air. Eliza spun around, her eyes widening as she saw Eric outside, writhing in pain.

"What the heck?" Eric squinted up at the doorway, his body jerking slightly from the unexpected shock. Eliza rummaged in her purse, pulled out her glasses, and slid them onto her face.

"Well, what's going on? Why don't you come in?" she urged.

"I can't. Your door's zapping me like crazy," Eric admitted, his expression a mix of confusion and annoyance.

Stepping out of her apartment and then re-entering, Eliza tested the waters herself. She passed through without any shock. At first, she dismissed it as a harmless static shock – you know, the kind you get from rubbing against certain fabrics. But as Eric followed her in, a burst of purple electricity danced across his skin, the sight bewildering both of them.

"Maybe it's your shorts and the ocean water or something," she suggested.

"Sure, that must be it," Eric cleared his throat, his discomfort evident. "I guess I'll catch you later." He scratched his head, retreating down the stairs toward his car.

"Thanks for coming! Had a blast!" Eliza shouted after him, though it seemed he wasn't really listening, offering a thumbs-up as he went. "Well, whatever."

Shutting her door, she turned around to find Jared watching her, his gaze unwavering.

"Your mom came over to put a charm on your place," he informed her casually.

"Charm? What's that?" Eliza asked, intrigued.

"I filled her in on the mystic incident. She swung by to make sure the place is protected from any bad vibes by adding a charm."

"Wow, I'll have to thank her for that," Eliza said, placing her things on the kitchen table.

"Also, your friend, he's a mystic," Jared added, trailing behind her.

Could that be why Eric couldn't enter her place? The pieces started to fall into place in Eliza's mind.

Every time something good happened to Eliza, her mom or Jared just had to swoop in and rain on her parade. The happiness she felt would fizzle away, leaving her feeling deflated.

Now, it was Jared's turn to play matchmaker, attempting to sabotage a potential romantic interest. But Eliza was having none of it. She rolled her eyes and grabbed a cheese stick from the fridge, munching on it to stave off the mounting irritation.

"I don't think Eric is some mystic, you know," she muttered to herself, her thoughts swirling. In the back of her head she knew Jared was right she planned to test it our herself.

"Seriously? You're gonna pretend I don't exist now, Eliza? Fine, go ahead and get yourself killed for all I care," Jared's voice was a mixture of annoyance and genuine concern.

"Jared, now is not the time," Eliza shot back, her patience wearing thin.

She decided against mentioning the bizarre encounter with the mermaids from the rave earlier. Jared would probably freak out and run to spill the beans to her mom. And that would only lead to one thing – her mom dragging her back home and forcing her to attend some community college nearby.

"How was the party? Anything weird happen? I need the deets, Eliza," Jared persisted.

Here we go, Eliza thought, bracing herself.

With a swift kick, Jared closed the front door and shuffled into the living room, the jingle of his necklace announcing his presence. Eliza settled onto the couch, firing up the TV. Finding the Netflix app, she resumed her episode of Pretty Little Liars, sinking into the familiar drama. Crossing her legs, she fixed her gaze on the screen.

"I've seen that guy before. Just can't remember where," Jared mused, his whiskers drooping thoughtfully.

"Jeez, chill out. I'll spill if you stop bugging me," Eliza replied, munching on her snack.

She knew if she didn't give him more information, Jared would leap to conclusions – probably assuming she'd been attacked by some mystical being. And well, she had been, though that just confirmed his point about avoiding large crowds. Honestly, she was already feeling worn out and drained from the day's events.

Eliza had no interest in receiving a lecture right now, so she opted for a casual response. "The party was surprisingly fun," she said with a practiced smile, masking her true feelings.

Later on, she retreated upstairs for a quick rejuvenating shower. Wrapped in her cardigan, she took a deep breath and hesitated before addressing her cat, who was busy grooming himself. "Jare?" she called.

His ears perked up, and he glanced her way. "Yeah?"

"Did you happen to be at the party? Like, were you there?"

Jared paused, his expression thoughtful. "Nah, I was here, helping your mom with some cleaning. Why do you ask?"

"Just curious. You weren't around when I left," Eliza replied, her voice casual.

Jared's gaze dropped, and a strange tension seemed to fill the room, casting an awkward vibe between them. As Eliza settled herself onto her comfy blanket, exhaustion tugging at her, she couldn't help but wonder: If it wasn't Eric who'd saved her and her mom wasn't present, then who was that mysterious figure in the water? Letting the thoughts drift away, she closed her eyes and allowed herself to succumb to sleep on the couch.

It was a quiet Sunday morning, and Eliza decided to dive into a bit of studying using the family grimoire. She reached under her bed, and just as she did, Jared swung the window open with his typical feline grace and hopped onto her bed. Finally locating the dark purple grimoire, she eagerly flipped it open.

With the tip of her index finger, Eliza turned the brittle, brown pages until she landed in the section dedicated to mystics. Among the entries, she discovered a whole array of topics, including an explanation about what a broomstick truly was.

As it turned out, it wasn't just a mode of transport – it was a versatile weapon capable of morphing into other deadly forms. The text revealed that it wouldn't respond until her transformation was fully complete, but frustratingly, it offered no clues on how to speed up that process.

Eliza reached into her purse and pulled out the broomstick, giving the button a tap. The metallic sound rang out as it reshaped itself in her hand, silver lines starting to emit a soft, ethereal glow. Memories of her mom using the broomstick flooded her mind – she could vividly recall the daggers flanking it, designed to aid in taking down mystics.

Flipping through the pages, Eliza stumbled upon a section that outlined strategies to defeat different types of mystics. Her eyes widened when she came across a picture of a mermaid that eerily resembled the ones she'd encountered on the beach. A shiver raced down her spine at the thought.

"Must be taken down in the water or with salt," Eliza read aloud. The realization hit her – the empty bottles her mom had strategically placed out during a moment of panic had been meant for this purpose. "Well, that beach is officially off-limits," she muttered to herself, her lips forming a determined line.

"Huh?" Jared glanced up from his playful antics with a furry ball on the floor. Eliza shot him a fleeting look before returning her attention to the book. Turning the page, she was met with an image of a man dressed in sleek black attire, his tousled dirty blonde hair falling just so. A mask concealed his mouth, but his piercing light brown eyes seemed to bore right into her.

Wait a second, Eliza thought, her heart racing. She'd seen this guy before...

He had featured in one of her dreams. A gasp escaped her lips as she stared at the image, and below it, she noticed hastily scrawled handwriting.

Alec Verel. Don't put trust in male witches in general... They're extremely dangerous.

While engrossed in her reading, Eliza noticed an odd phenomenon – the man in the image appeared to be walking in place. Intrigued, she fixed her gaze more intently upon the picture, only to watch as he gradually quickened his pace until he was running in place.

The black hood of his attire swirled around him as if carried by an invisible wind. Eliza leaned forward, disbelief prompting her to investigate further, to ascertain whether her eyes were playing tricks on her.

As she strained to get a better view, a sudden surge of heat seemed to pierce her eyes, and instinctively, they slammed shut in response.

"Eliza!" Jared's voice pierced the air, a note of urgency ringing in his call.

☆☆☆

Suddenly, Eliza found herself in the middle of a vast grassy field, the world around her shifting and changing.

Startled, she sat up, her eyes widening as the man from the picture came into view. He was hot on the heels of someone, tearing across the vibrant green landscape and disappearing into the dense woods.

With an intense burst of energy, he leaped effortlessly onto the low-hanging branches, disappearing into the forest canopy. Driven by an inexplicable impulse, Eliza took off after him, her hair billowing behind her like a living thing.

"Mellissa!" His cry pierced the air, carrying a mix of urgency and longing. "Mellissa!" His voice echoed once more, as if urging him to reach her before it was too late. And he moved with an astonishing speed, like a blur racing forward.

Finally, Eliza managed to close the gap between them. The pursued girl dashed past a tree, her vibrant red hair trailing like a comet's tail. She was dressed in a matching black outfit, exuding an air of confidence.

Her tight leather shorts and long top flowed with her movements, and a sleek tail completed her ensemble. Abruptly halting, she swung her legs around with grace, landing a swift jab against the guy's chest. The scene played out before Eliza, a vivid display of tension and emotion that left her heart racing.

In a quick smash, the man slammed into a tree. Melissa clicked her broomstick's button and it grew longer, with daggers poking out like her mom's stick. Swirly lines wrapped around it, making a scraping noise as it finished changing.

Melissa rushed toward him. Clicking the button again, one end turned into a silver sword. She swung it in the air, aiming at the guy.

Eliza realized she'd seen this woman in the grimoire – her great grandmother.

Hiding behind a tree, Eliza watched the fight unfold.

"Listen to me, Mellissa!" the man shouted, dodging her attacks. He used his broomstick to block her sword. The blades made a loud clang when they clashed.

"You're a traitor!" Melissa snapped, her sword coming down.

The man grabbed her arm to stop her. She kneed him in the gut. Then she slashed at his cheek, making him bleed. She held her blade up, ready for his next move, her eyes narrow and focused.

"I saw you talking to that mystic. How dare you persuade him into talking to Lauren?" Melissa's voice hissed with anger.

"He was helping me. You must understand, Mellissa," the man pleaded, his gaze lifting to meet hers.

"You were helping him corrupt my family! Who knows what could be transferred down our bloodline, generation to generation," she cried out, her distress evident.

A swift, forceful movement followed – her fist lashed out at him. Yet, he was quicker, catching her wrist and effectively throwing her to the ground, their bodies colliding as he fell on top of her. With practiced determination, he pinned her down, his breathing ragged.

"You must understand," he said, his words a breathless plea. "He saw your pregnant daughter talking to a corrupt elf," he explained. Mellissa's struggles halted abruptly, her eyes locked onto him, her disbelief evident.

"Lauren?"

Lauren, Eliza's recently deceased grandmother, was Mellissa's daughter.

"Lauren would not do such a thing," Melissa declared, her voice heavy with incredulity. "She couldn't have," she added, her voice filled with denial.

"I was talking to him to help you, Mellissa. I was finding out information," he huffed, his efforts focused on restraining her. "You must stop the pregnancy."

"Let go of me, Alec!" Melissa's voice surged with anger and desperation.

"Listen to me! If you don't stop this, her child—"

Before he could finish his sentence, Mellissa managed to break free from his grip. Swiftly, she twisted her body and delivered a resounding headbutt that caught him off guard.

"You're a liar, Alec Verel," Melissa snapped, her words dripping with contempt. "The Verel family will all be sent to Ravamere to die."

Eliza watched with a mix of unease and anticipation as Melissa's fury radiated through her gaze. The sharp sound of metal scraping met her ears, a precursor to Melissa's action. In a swift motion, she clicked the button on her broomstick.

☆☆☆

Eliza felt like she might hurl, her stomach churning with unease. Blinking her eyes open, she grabbed at her bed sheets, trying to steady herself. It was as if her insides were doing a dance she hadn't signed up for. Her heart raced like a trapped bird, and a gnarly headache throbbed to life. She tried to piece together what had happened.

Could any of that crazy stuff actually be real?

Pushing past the queasiness, Eliza focused on the task at hand. She forced her eyes open wider, as if that could clear her foggy mind. It was a struggle to keep her thoughts straight, but she couldn't just let this slide. She needed answers, pronto.

Her book beckoned to her, its pages whispering secrets she needed to unravel. She flipped it open, her heart pounding in anticipation. It was like talking to a long-lost friend, hoping for a bit of wisdom to drop in her lap.

"Okay, great grandma. I'm seriously lost here. Give me something, anything," she mumbled, her words like a plea to the universe. Almost on cue, the pages shuffled, guiding her to a section labeled "Verel."

"Nice timing," Eliza said aloud, her voice carrying a mix of surprise and gratitude. She skimmed the words, absorbing the info like a sponge soaking up water after a long run.

"The Verel, huh? Evil male witches playing a dark game, teaming up with messed-up mystics. Some mystics are okay, but others are diving headfirst into the dark side. And they're not just dipping their toes – they're corrupt to the core. These Verel guys pick a female witch to keep their wicked line going, and eventually, they do away with her. Just like a messed-up mystic, it's like a twisted thrill for them – killing innocents or twisting them into shadows. And guess what? Joining forces with female witches gives these Verel dudes a power-up, since their offspring keep the evil flowing. But hold up, not all male witches are bad news. Some might have good intentions, but for now, best to tread carefully."

A note added a dash of emphasis: "Don't trust the Verel."

"Eliza! What's happening?" Jared's voice cut through the air, laced with worry. Eliza was lost in the book's words, but his concern couldn't be ignored.

"What's up?" His tone was urgent, and Eliza could practically feel his eyes drilling into her back.

With a shaky voice, Eliza finally replied, "It's about my dad... I need to know more about his death."

Jared's brow furrowed in concentration, his struggle to remember evident in his frustrated expression. It was a common struggle, but that didn't make it any less aggravating.

"I can't remember all the details. It was some accident, and your mom was somehow involved," he admitted, his voice tinged with irritation.

"Yeah..." Eliza's voice trailed off as she looked around the room, her thoughts wandering.

"Are you okay? Something feels off," Jared's concern was palpable.

Eliza sighed and met his gaze. "Was my dad connected to mystics?" The question hung heavy in the air, laden with implications she was afraid to consider.

"And who's this Verel?" Impatience colored Eliza's voice as she fired off another question.

Jared hesitated, his gaze darting away as he scratched his nose.

"How did you... Where did you...?" His words stumbled, his urgency clear. "The book, the grimoire. Where is it, Eliza?" His demand was sharp, and before she could react, he leapt off the bed, landing gracefully on the floor.

Swiftly flipping open the book's pages with a paw, he sought out the message about the Verel. With a determined move, he tore the page out, his teeth slicing through the paper in one swift motion.

"What in the world are you doing?" Eliza's voice rang out in shock.

"Stop! You're not supposed to be poking around in this alone," Jared's tone was sharp, almost angry.

"But—"

"Eliza, this book is a whole lot of dark and twisty that you're not ready for," he snapped back, his eyes serious. "You're a rookie in this mystical world, and you can't predict how you'll handle certain revelations. Remember your mom's words? Being in transformation mode makes you a magnet for mystics, especially if you're stumbling upon new intel." His words held authority. "And you can't have missed the heightened senses—better eyesight, hearing, agility."

His teeth clamped down on the book's binding, and in a fluid motion, he leaped onto the windowsill. He gingerly set the book down, placing a paw on its cover and leveling his gaze with hers. "These changes take time to settle in fully. When you're ready, you'll know what to do."

"Jared, please! I need your help," Eliza's voice quivered as tears gathered in her eyes. "This is all so overwhelming, and I'm drowning in confusion. I just need answers to anchor me, to make sense of everything."

"I get that it's a lot to take in, but I'm just trying to—"

"Jared! You've been keeping so much from me," she said, her voice breaking under the weight of her emotions.

"I know that all of this is a tsunami of emotions, trust me..."

"How could you possibly understand? You're a cat," Eliza's voice wavered, a mix of frustration and despair.

Jared's ears drooped, his whiskers bristled, and his eyes narrowed in sadness. He stared at the floor, a heavy weight in his expression.

"I might not have all my memories," he began, his gaze lifting to meet hers, "but one thing I do remember is that the Verel transformed your brother into a cat."

12

— . —

Epilogue

The carnival lights beamed off my skin. I glanced down slowly, hearing the roars of people. I pressed my back against the cold hard wall behind me. The sound of my slight breathing, entered my ears. I feel my hair whip away from my face. There's footsteps walking toward me. Eliza's been gone, and I don't where she's been. I've tried calling her cell, but she keeps ignoring me for some reason. The glare from my cellular device reflects my eyes.

"Dawn you're up in five."

I turn to look at my stage manager. "You got it Bryan." I breathe in from my nostrils and tuck the cellphone into my dance bag. I stop for a second, harsh breathing sounds from the darkness in front of me again. I really hope this wasn't another one of those mystics Eliza told me about.

My hairs grown longer since the last time I've seen Liza, she disappeared and left a note on the table. All I remember the day she disappear is her saying.

Going to an art show with Donovan.

That was like three weeks ago, I feel my heart begin to thump just thinking if she's all right. I've notified the police as soon as she didn't return. I remember feeling my lips quiver in pain and sadness, only because I thought one of them actually got to her, the mystics. Ever since that day I've been pushing back that horrible thought for some time now.

I just don't want anything to cloud my judgements or become reckless, who knows, maybe I'm next on the list? I've always been by her side no matter what, even if I thought it was a little weird that her and her mother thought they were witches. Yes, every friend just as myself would have her back and not judge. I have to admit I was a little scared for them both if anyone had figured their secret. How could anyone trust a human like me? I'm clumsy and a wreck, but Eliza needed me she needed an anchor, and so I was just that for her.

Only until one of the guys I planned to hook up with turned out to be a mystical creature, who instead, wanted me for my innocence and purity or whatever attracts them the most. I guess I wasn't really there for her at that moment, but she was there for me. It was that night when Jared, her talking cat, and Eliza saved me. It was then when I figured having a best friend who's a witch-kicking butt-assassin killer, couldn't be so bad.

The bass from outside bumps on my back and chest. I know I have my routine down, I've practiced it a billion of times. Bryan walks from around the corner, I glance behind him at the Ferris wheel circling slowly. I happen to pick up the slightest movement from behind me, I don't turn around though, I need to keep it together. A crowd is waiting for my performance. I press my lips and narrow my eyes at him. Raising my hands, I pull the rest of my pink hair over my shoulders; the ends pass my light blue crop top and tickle my skin. Strutting by Bryan he rolls his eyes.

"Don't screw up." I hear him say, scribbling on his clipboard.

I scrunch my hair with my fingers and look out at the bouncing group. "I never screw up."

Smiling I skip out from the darkness as mist from above sprinkles on me. It's glitter I feel from the tiny colorful pieces. I body roll toward center stage, glance down and then snap my head back with the beat.

Tick, tick, tock my hips sway from left to right. The guys in front of me scream into my ears, I feel their hands reaching up my legs. Horny and pathetic, wanting something more from me. It's always these kinds of guys who try and hit me up each time after a performance. I can't help but use the vibe to excel my performing methods even better.

I twirl around, showing them my back and dropping down to the floor on my knees. I bite on my lips, holding back my smile and breathing in the crisp drunk wind. The lights always keep me moving, they're the only thing that fuels me and helps the nerves. Everything is quiet, just like inside a forest, hearing a stream run nearby and the tiny bubbles popping against the moist rocks, and the crickets rubbing their legs creating their beautiful melodies. It's soothing and calming, this is how I think of the stage.

Dancing is my life.

I pump my arms up and pop my chest. Bryan is watching me and taking notes. I give him a quick wink as I turn back around to face my crowd. The tins of paint turn slowly outward to the boys and girls. I bounce with my walk, kicking one tin. Paint sprays up into the dark magenta sky. Immediately the other tins explode, painting at my crowd. I snap my fingers, stepping back slowly and moving with the beat. I close my eyes, waiting for the paint to pour down on me.

Whenever I'm down in the dumps...this place brings me back to life.

"Dawn, Dawn, Dawn!" The guys scream my name, I wipe the paint from my eyes. I open them at the boy's mouths gaped and their veins outlined on the sides of their necks; their abs and jaws all smothered in colorful paint. My knee pads grind on me, they're too tight. I keep my act going and then glance at the DJ. He points at his invisible watch, my time is up. I probably only made four hundred tonight. My hands move down passed my breasts and along my sides. I smear the paint on my skin, I jump up and down, twirl one more time and strut backstage.

"You went over by a few minutes." Bryan looks at me from his clipboard. "Ashlyn you're up."

Ashlyn's ashy blonde hair whipped the side of my neck as she jogged out on stage. The crowd sounded louder as soon as she hit the stage. The claps from the bass pinched my ears.

I hold out my hand for my pay tonight. I feel the crisp paper in my palm's grip. Licking the tip of my thumb, I finger through counting. I lift my eyes at Bryan.

"This is only two hundred..."

"Like I said you went over your time."

"I was supposed to make four hundred tonight." He ignores me and walks down the ramp on the side of the stage. "Ashlyn always goes over...and not just by a couple of minutes

"Bryan! Are you serious?" He ignores me and talks to the stage crew.

Jackass.

I tuck my lingering hairs behind my right ear. Slouching over to my dance bag, I pull out my phone to see if Eliza ever called me back.

I tap my phones screen, but it's dead. This is an everyday thing, checking messages and nothing, always nothing. I roll my eyes and huff my bag around my arm.

"I can give you an extra two hundred." A guy walks out from the darkness, his blue-grey eyes glimmered down at me. His black blazer and clean white crisped undershirt, was tucked nicely in his denim shorts. I noticed his white converses and the tattoo on the side of his claves.

"I've seen you dance and wouldn't mind paying you extra." He bites on his bottom lip.

This guy was obviously a stalker, who would hide backstage in the dark? I turned the other way around and walked toward the ramp down the stage. So not interested.

Jared said the only reason why mystics were attracted to me was because of my innocence. The metal steps I walk down cling against my boots, hearing the ding from each step I make helps me forget about Jare and Liza. I land on dirt and hear the crumbles from my shoes crunching on the gravel. I walk by a girl hugging a huge teddy bear, and getting on her tippy toes to kiss her boyfriend. She's happy and the vibe rubs off of me, I can never have what she has. Guys only want one thing from Dawn Roberts, and it sure isn't love. Sticking my hands into my pockets, I shove my way through the crowd.

Plus, who am I to look attractive? I mean I'm covered in paint. Glass breaks next to me, I twist to my left, witnessing a guy blow out a pyramid of glass bottles.

"I won! Shweet."

"Honey I want that white bear?" His girlfriend whines.

"What bear? I'm getting a new basketball from my win." He licks his lips and forms a fist. The girl immediately slapped his arm. I shake my head, and turn around at the guy I saw backstage. My face pretty much crashed into something fluffy.

Donald duck's beak poked between my eyes.

"I just thought I'd get you something. I promise I wasn't stalking you." He raised his hands in the air with his palms faced out to me as if he comes in peace. I glanced down, pressing my lips together.

"What's wrong?"

I lift my droopy gaze at the guy. "Donald is ruined with my paint." I hear the guy chuckle at me. "You're still a stalker," I say, snatching the prize he won for me, walking toward the parking lot. "Did you just steal my prize?"

"Sure did!" I walk up to the edge of the curb, seeing a long limousine. "Plus you won it for me anyway..." I say looking up at him.

The driver steps out and opens the door. "Corey are you ready sir?" I lift up my index finger and point at myself. The driver grins and shakes his head. "Oh...Uh."

I point at the guy next me, and then point at the fancy vehicle. I place one of my hands on my hips. I release a huff sound and say, "who are you?" I cross my arms, staring at this Corey guy next to me.

"I can take you home if you'd like? I'd rather have you get my car dirty with your paint instead." He walks toward the car and slides in. I glance over at my raggedy car and then back to the limousine.

"No it's fine, thanks though." I chuck up the deuces.

"I have...food." He says, poking his head out of the sunroof. I slowly turn around and glare at him. A girl can't say no to food.

What if this guy turns out to be a mystic? I shake off the thought, I've learned enough from Eliza to be able to kick his ass by myself.

Milton Keynes UK
Ingram Content Group UK Ltd.
UKHW010710040923
428018UK00014B/913

9 781944 253813